"Jed, what are you doing?" Rae asked.

"I'm stuck on you."

"You're what!"

"My cufflink is tangled in your dress." He lifted his hand away to show her, and the sequinned bodice gaped open, exposing even more of the creamy flesh of her back.

"Don't do that!" she exclaimed, pushing her dress back into place.

"You're no fun," he complained. "Think of it as a peek-a-boo dress."

"Sure, one peek and you say 'boo.' "

"I'd never boo," he promised. "Now let's get you unstuck."

He moved closer to her then and Rae felt an electrifying charge jolt her. Jed's gaze grew hot and color grazed his cheekbones.

"Jed," she whispered. Then his mouth covered hers, and she was lost. . . .

WHAT ARE *LOVESWEPT* ROMANCES?

They are stories of true romance and touching emotion. We believe those two very important ingredients are constants in our highly sensual and very believable stories in the *LOVESWEPT* line. Our goal is to give you, the reader, stories of consistently high quality that may sometimes make you laugh, sometimes make you cry, but are always fresh and creative and contain many delightful surprises within their pages.

Most romance fans read an enormous number of books. Those they truly love, they keep. Others may be traded with friends and soon forgotten. We hope that each *LOVESWEPT* romance will be a treasure—a "keeper." We will always try to publish

LOVE STORIES YOU'LL NEVER FORGET
BY AUTHORS YOU'LL ALWAYS REMEMBER

The Editors

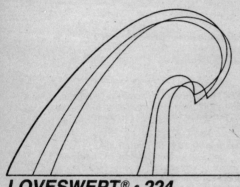

LOVESWEPT® • 224

Linda Cajio
Double Dealing

BANTAM BOOKS
TORONTO • NEW YORK • LONDON • SYDNEY • AUCKLAND

DOUBLE DEALING
A Bantam Book / December 1987

If you would be interested in receiving protective vinyl
covers for your Loveswept books, please write to this address
for information:

Loveswept
Bantam Books
P.O. Box 985
Hicksville, NY 11802

ISBN 0-553-21856-5

Published simultaneously in the United States and Canada

Bantam Books are published by Bantam Books, Inc. Its trademark, consisting of the words "Bantam Books" and the por-
trayal of a rooster, is Registered in U.S. Patent and Trademark
Office and in other countries. Marca Registrada. Bantam
Books, Inc., 666 Fifth Avenue, New York, New York 10103.

PRINTED IN THE UNITED STATES OF AMERICA

O   0 9 8 7 6 5 4 3 2 1

For Shirley, who taught me that "Life is a banquet and most poor suckers are starving to death." Many thanks and much love. I'm feasting now.

One

Breaking and entering was easier than he had expected.

Jed Waters immediately corrected his exaggeration as he jumped down from the top of the six-foot wrought-iron fence that surrounded the Barkeley estate. He was only trespassing—and in broad daylight. Hell, he thought. Whatever the label for the crime, it was still no way for a vice president of Atlantic Developers to earn a living. But then old Merriman Barkeley always had said eccentricity was the spice of life. He'd proven that long ago. He was the only member of Philadelphia's premier Main Line family who insisted on living across the Delaware River in New Jersey. Unfortunately, Merriman's latest eccentricity had been a whopper, and it was costing Atlantic a good deal of time, money, and aggravation. Jed hoped a sensible discussion would correct the matter with a minimum of fuss. The trick, though, was to get Merriman to agree to talk. So far, the old man had neatly eluded all phone calls and letters from the company's lawyers.

Never do business with friends or family, or certifiable crackpots, Jed reminded himself for the tenth time as he absently touched his mustache. He'd forgotten that Merriman qualified on the first and last counts.

Pushing aside the thick branches of a holly tree, he surveyed the two acres of green lawn that fronted the majestic old Georgian mansion. Satisfied that no human being marred the pastoral scene, Jed continued on his mission. Breaking into a half trot, he followed the line of holly trees which served as a windbreak on three sides of the estate. The Delaware River bordered the fourth. He chuckled. Trespassing beat the hell out of having to trim all four hundred and twenty-three holly trees on a steamy summer afternoon. As a teenager, he'd done that more times than he cared to remember, working at the estate for his father's landscaping business.

His amusement was replaced by a grimace. Trimming an endless row of holly trees beat the hell out of what he was about to do next, though.

"Barkeley never did make things easy," Jed muttered out loud. He sighed in relief, as he glimpsed the first of the boxwood shrubs that bordered the old-fashioned garden maze. Situated on the left side of the property, the maze encompassed a full acre. It was Merriman's pride and joy. It was also the easiest way to get to the house without being seen.

He kept to the cover of the trees until he was

opposite the maze entrance. Grateful that the holly leaves were still soft, he pushed his way in between the trees. There was only about a hundred feet of open space between him and the maze. He knew the other entrance was just a few yards from the side terrace. If he'd timed it exactly right, Merriman would be having afternoon tea on the terrace, a ritual the old man performed rain or shine, from the first of March to the end of November, claiming it was good for the lungs. The raw October day would hardly deter him.

Jed hoped he remembered the way through the maze. He'd been seventeen the last time he'd gone through it. Eighteen years was a long time between mazes.

Taking a deep breath, he ran across the lawn and into the maze. As high boxwoods enclosed him in a shaded corridor, he grinned to himself. Piece of ca—

His self-congratulations went no further, as his ears caught the unmistakable sounds of someone rushing across the grass. He glanced over his shoulder and saw two enormous dogs racing toward him, their jaws open and tongues lolling. Instantly deciding there was only one sensible recourse, he turned and ran for all he was worth deeper into the maze. So much for a smooth entry, he thought. His brain scrambled to dredge up the maze's "key." Two right, one left, double back and turn right . . .

Skidding to an abrupt halt, he gazed in shock at the barrier of solid hedge where there was supposed to be an open corridor. Cursing himself for his mistake, he whipped around just in time to see the two Great Danes enter the outer end of the corridor. They began barking furiously as they closed in on their quarry. He slowly backed away from them. Muscles tensed for fight or flight, he wished he knew what the standing-high-jump record was. He had a feeling he was about to break it.

The huge animals stalked purposively toward him, their growls coming from deep in their massive chests, their fangs glistening. Jed pressed back into the wall of boxwood. In spite of the fifty-degree temperature, sweat trickled down his temples. Ignoring the well-trimmed branches stabbing at his flesh, he tried to press straight through to the other side.

"Hello," said a pleasantly low, feminine voice from the other end of the corridor. "Were you looking for someone?"

"Just admiring the view," Jed snapped, never glancing away from the dogs to see who he was talking to.

"It is a beautiful sight, isn't it?" agreed the woman. "Well, I'll leave you to it—"

"I'm quite willing to admit I'm trespassing," Jed interrupted coolly. "Call the mutts off, and I'll go quietly. Believe me, I'll be more than happy to go quietly."

There was a long silence. Jed wished he'd seen the Grand Canyon just once . . . watched the sun set on the Pyramids before the sun set on him . . .

"Samson! Delilah! Watch!"

At the sharp command, the dogs instantly became silent. They sat down on their haunches and looked around in bewilderment, like a couple of drunk dachshunds. Still eyeing them, Jed cautiously allowed his body to relax. He risked a glance in his rescuer's direction, as she came to stand behind the dogs.

Gazing into questioning green-gray eyes, he completely forgot about the vicious animals sitting practically at his feet. He knew those eyes, and the deep midnight-black hair. Nobody could ever forget the exotic combination. The waif-like little girl he remembered was now a woman . . . a beautiful woman with the delicate features of a cameo portrait, except for the smear of mud she had across a creamy cheek, and her hair falling out of its fastening. The burgundy Shaker sweater and faded jeans covering the slender but very feminine curves were also mud-splattered. So were the unappealing Wellington boots. Somehow, though, her attire didn't seem at all out of place with her beautiful face and form. Jed wasn't surprised by the thought. Rachel Barkeley always had liked to play in the mud.

Thanking his Maker for little girls, he crossed his arms over his chest and smiled.

"You've grown up, Rae."

In dismay, Rachel Honoria Barkeley stared at the man posed nonchalantly at the maze wall. There'd been a time when she considered Jed Waters a big brother, but she knew he was here now for a very unbrotherly reason. It had been a shock to discover that her childhood friend had almost conned a sweet and slightly crazy old man into allowing the Barkeley Estate to be turned into a marina-condominium complex. Almost, she thought with satisfaction. Uncle Merry had finally had the common sense to pull out of the sale and return the down payment.

Rae studied the self-assured stranger who was so different from the shy adolescent she remembered so well. Jed's physical appearance only enhanced the man he had become. His carrot-colored hair had faded to a deep auburn, and his features were more rugged and sharply defined. The thick reddish-brown mustache made him look even more virile. His hazel eyes were as striking as ever, but there was an experienced quality to his gaze now. He had to be over six feet tall—certainly a good head taller than her five feet eight inches. His lithe, muscular frame was accentuated by the jeans and baseball jacket he wore.

For a brief moment, Rae wondered how the dogs would have fared if she'd left them to their job. Being intimidated by a couple of Great Danes was not a trait of a fast-rising corporate vice president. Even at their friendliest, Samson and Delilah sent most people into a panic, but Jed had simply stood his ground and glared at them.

Realizing she was far too interested in him as a man, she turned her attention to the purpose of his visit. Why she had expected Atlantic Developers to just drop their plans for the complex after they lost the sale, she didn't know. Wishful thinking probably. She reminded herself that she hadn't reached the age of twenty-seven without learning how to stand her ground too. Jed was in for a surprise if he thought the new owner of the estate was as pliable as her Uncle Merry. Images of bulldozers ripping up the beautiful two-hundred-year-old house and grounds ran through her head, and she suppressed a shudder. The estate's first owner had been her ancestor, Samuel Barkeley. The estate had passed out of the family during the 1800's, but it had finally been brought back into Barkeley hands by Uncle Merry. And there it would stay, she promised herself.

She decided the best way to deal with a representative of Atlantic was to act as cool and nonchalant as he did. Being covered in mud was a distinct disadvantage, but she forced herself to ignore her appearance. It was just bad luck that he had arrived when she'd been attempting to locate a broken water line. Anyway, Jed certainly wasn't dressed in a regulation three-piece Brooks Brothers suit.

"Most people do grow up, Jed," she said finally, shoving her hands into the pockets of her jeans. "You certainly have."

"It's really good to see you again, Rae." Smiling, Jed took two steps toward her. Instantly alert, the dogs growled a warning at him. He stepped back against the boxwoods again.

"The old place hasn't changed much," he commented in a very dry voice.

Rae smiled politely to cover her amusement at his casual attitude. "Oh, a few things have."

"I see someone is still stuck with the job of trimming the holly trees," he added.

"Not as nicely as you did," she assured him. "You should have come up to the house, Jed."

"I just thought I'd take a look around first."

"Not a very smart thing to do."

"I guess not," he drawled, then pointed to the dogs who growled again. "How do you turn these two off?"

Rae grinned. "You don't 'turn off' Great Danes, Jed, you just hope for the best."

"Then let's hope for the best, shall we?"

She shrugged. "Heel!"

Without a glance at their prey, the dogs rose and circled around until they stood next to her. They butted their heads against her thighs in search of affection. Rae absently fondled Samson's ears, then Delilah's, as she watched Jed walk toward her.

He scowled at the dogs as they settled back on their haunches. "What the hell do you feed them, anyway? A side of beef laced with megavitamins?"

"Seems like it sometimes," she said with a chuckle. "Actually, they're just healthy."

"A Doberman is healthy, Rae. These two are the Arnold Schwarzeneggers of the dog kingdom."

"Well, you won't have to deal with them much longer—"

"Are they going on a doggie break?" he asked hopefully.

She burst into laughter. Jed gave the dogs a last look of disgust, then grinned at her. She managed to subdue her mirth enough to say, "What I meant was, you'll have to leave now."

He raised his eyebrows. "I will?"

"Much as I would like to visit with you, I have a broken water line to fix—"

"I wondered where the mud came from."

"And I have to get back to it," she finished. She refused to apologize for her appearance. Rather, she congratulated herself on her poise. It was evident that Jed had been trying to throw her off balance with casual conversation, before broaching the subject of the estate.

"Actually, Rae, I came to see Merriman."

She stared at him in confusion. "Merriman?"

"Yes. Merriman."

He wasn't making any sense, she thought. When her uncle had informed Atlantic that the estate was no longer for sale, surely he'd also told them. . .

"You came to see Uncle Merry?" she asked carefully, interrupting her own thoughts.

Jed frowned, suddenly looking like the boy she remembered. "Your uncle, yes. Look, Rae, I'll be honest. Merriman agreed to sell the estate to the company I work for, Atlantic Developers—"

"I know that," she broke in.. "But why . . ." Her voice trailed off, when a horrible thought occurred. "Oh, my God! He did send back the money, didn't he?"

"Obviously, you do know something about it," he said. "The company refused the return of the down payment. We negotiated in good faith, and Merriman signed the agreement of sale. We expect him to honor that agreement, Rae. Much as I like him, someone's got to talk some sense into him. He can't just go around signing agreements and backing out—"

"It wouldn't be the first time," she muttered out loud, realizing that someone had slipped up somewhere. If Jed was intent on seeing her uncle, as he obviously was, then that meant he and Atlantic Developers didn't know about the estate's recent change of ownership. She took a sure guess at who had neglected to tell them. Just as he had neglected to tell her Atlantic had refused to take back their down payment. "That dirty, miserable, sneaky old . . . coot!"

At her angry outburst, the dogs growled menacingly. Jed just raised his eyebrows and waited for an explanation.

"My uncle," she pronounced in a disgusted tone, more than willing to trade years of love for the opportunity to strangle him, "has not only renounced all worldly pleasures, he's also renounced his last hold on his sanity! The damn fool never told me Atlantic refused the down payment before he left—"

"What!"

"And he obviously didn't tell Atlantic that the reason he changed his mind on the sale was because he deeded the estate to me."

Jed staggered backward, as if someone had thrown him a right to the chin. His eyes widened in disbelief.

Rae nodded her head.

"Two days ago, Uncle Merry 'retired' into a monastery. I own the estate now."

Two

"A *monastery!*"

A thousand questions and demands ran through Jed's brain. He tried to sort them into some semblance of order.

"A monastery!"

Rae nodded again. "Not any old monastery, mind you. One that's somewhere in the Himalayan foothills of Nepal. He's totally inaccessible, and I bet he planned it that way."

"Nepal!" he shouted, waving his hands in the air. He immediately realized yelling was useless, and forced himself to calm down. "I don't believe it."

"Neither do I," she agreed, shaking her head. "This place was supposed to be free and clear. Wait until I get a hold of Uncle Merry—"

"You own the estate!" he exclaimed in dawning realization. He was still confused and shocked by Merriman's vanishing act, and Rae's words were just beginning to sink in. "That's impossible. We had an agreement of sale with your uncle. It's still valid."

"I doubt it," she said.

"But he couldn't have sold it to you. Not with the agreement of sale as an outstanding lien against the property!"

Rae smiled. "But he didn't sell it to me, Jed. He deeded it to me. As a gift."

"A gift!" he shouted. He didn't even bother to try and calm himself this time. "Who the hell gives away a two-million-dollar estate as a damn gift?"

"Uncle Merry," she replied calmly. "Although I feel as if I've been given a Trojan horse."

"Then give it back." Jed ground his teeth together at the thought of what Atlantic's president would say when he told him their reluctant seller was in a monastery in Nepal. This was the damnedest stunt Merriman had ever pulled . . .

"Oh, I couldn't possibly give it back," Rae said sweetly, breaking in on his thoughts. "Uncle Merry wanted me to have it."

He glared at her. "Well, he had no legal right to deed it to you. Any court will uphold the agreement of sale, and I have to tell you, Rae, Atlantic will sue. The company has put a good deal of time and money into the plans for the marina complex. I'm sure you'd like to avoid spending years in litigation with the company—"

"But why would Atlantic sue me?" she asked, a very innocent look in her eyes. "Your problem is with Uncle Merry. Frankly, I wouldn't blame you a bit if you and your company took him all the way to the Supreme Court. Really, you should. I love my uncle very much, but he pulled a dirty trick on you by not completely clearing up the agreement of sale before he deeded the place to me. I suggest you call his lawyers and inform them of the problem. I have no idea why they didn't inform your company of the situation in the first place." Shaking her head, she began to walk down the maze corridor. "Negligent of them, I must say."

He reached out and took her wrist to stop her. Instantly two sets of canine teeth closed gently around his arm. He looked down to discover Samson and Delilah gazing up at him almost gleefully. He let go of Rae, and the dogs let go of him. He smiled at her. "Be sensible, Rae, and realize that if Atlantic has to sue Merriman, you're sure to be named a co-defendant. Probably, a judge will order you to vacate the property while a decision is being reached. Neither of us really wants to make a bunch of lawyers rich over this—"

Anger flashed in her green-gray eyes, and he found himself momentarily forgetting all thoughts of lawsuits and lawyers. She had the most beautiful eyes, he decided absently.

"I told you, Jed. I'm very sympathetic, but I'm not involved in your company's dispute with my uncle. Call his lawyers. Uncle Merry can well afford to pay any settlement your company asks, especially now that he's given up his Dom Pérignon and beluga caviar. Now, if you'll excuse me, I have a broken water line to fix."

She turned and walked away, the dogs pacing beside her. Jed caught up to them and fell into step next to her.

"Nice try, Rae," he chided, as they retraced their way through the maze. "But you've got to be as crazy as Merriman, if you think you're not involved in this. The deed is now in your name. Probably illegally."

She gave him an appraising glance. "Personally, I think the only crazy one in this is you, Jed. How could you have been a part of a plan to plow the house under and replace it with hideous condos?"

"Very nice condominiums that would be in keeping with the gracious setting," he corrected, ignoring the face she made. "It's my job, Rae. And Atlantic planned to turn the mansion into a clubhouse for the complex."

"A clubhouse!" She shuddered. "Now I've heard everything. Atlantic wants to turn a piece of history into a clubhouse. And you would have let them . . ."

"Atlantic will see to it that the house retains its character," he told her in a cold tone. "Merriman insisted on that, and I would have too. This estate sits next to deep water, north of riverbank industries and Philly's busy shipping traffic. It's the most ideal spot for twenty miles to put up a marina and condo complex."

They emerged from the maze, and Rae pointed to an enormous shade tree about one hundred yards away on the front lawn. Its leaves were in full fall technicolor. "See that oak? When I was eight years old, I fell out of that tree and broke my arm."

"I remember," Jed said. "It happened the first summer I worked for my father."

"Then remember this. From the time I was five,

I spent every summer here with Uncle Merry. I learned to sail in that deep water you're so hepped up about. I slept in the same bed used by seven senators, ten congressmen, and three presidents. I learned to play the harp in the drawing room. I read the library's signed copies of *Poor Richard's Almanac* and *Sons and Lovers.* And I had my backside tanned for clipping off all the rose blossoms because I was playing Morticia Addams. I love this estate exactly the way it is, and I love the old man who let me be myself here." Her voice broke, and Jed felt an odd protectiveness wash through him. She drew a deep breath in an obvious attempt to control her emotions. "There's more than local heritage here. There's a personal one. Believe me, Jed. The last thing your company wants to do is drag me into their dispute with my uncle. The very last thing. Samson! Delilah! See the gentleman to the front gate!"

Without another word, Rachel Barkeley turned and disappeared back into the maze.

As he watched her go, Jed was tempted to give her beautiful backside another tanning. He owed her one. After all, she'd tried to blame *him* for lopping off all the roses. A helpless chuckle escaped him at the memory. That little witch hadn't changed at all. She was still feisty as hell, and still acting the innocent.

His amusement subsided when he remembered the mess Merriman had created over the estate. Obviously, Rae intended to fight a multimillion-dollar corporation, if she had to. He decided he'd have to do something to stop her. This wasn't Rachel Barkeley's fight.

He looked down at the dogs, who were waiting to see in which direction he moved.

"Let's go, guys," he said, beginning the long walk across the lawn to the front gate.

The dogs trailed behind him, clearly disappointed.

Rae was still muttering curses under her breath, when she reached the herb garden behind the house. The garden was planted in a fleur-de-lis pattern, and there was a white wooden gazebo at the bottom point. It was usually a beautiful sight year round, but mud created by the leaking irrigation line had been tracked throughout the planting bed and grass walkway of one section, ruining the effect.

"I have managed to cut off the water to this area, Miss Rachel," said a small man, as he looked up from the hole she'd dug earlier. His formal British accent was still strong, despite many years spent in the States.

"Thanks, Burrows," she said, and drew on a pair of filthy work gloves. She eyed her uncle's butler sourly, noting the spotless vinyl apron that covered his equally immaculate black suit. Even his "Wellies" were relatively mud-free. She'd never seen Burrows truly dirty and most likely never would. Knowing Burrows, he probably dipped himself in Scotchgard stain repeller every morning. "Have you called the plumbers? And if you tell me one more time that I'm too old to be digging in the dirt, I'll bean you with the shovel."

"Yes, miss, and the plumber shall arrive shortly."

"Which means next week," she muttered, wondering how the day could possibly get worse. Don't even consider it, she told herself. It might just happen.

She picked up a shovel and began clearing away more mud. Originally, she'd started the hole in order to assess the damage to the water line, but now she was grateful for the hard physical work. She didn't want to think about her confrontation with Jed.

Unfortunately, the matter was taken out of her hands when Burrows said, "This section of the garden will have to be replanted. It is a shame Mr. Waters, Senior, retired to Florida. He was very knowledgeable. I'm afraid the new lawn service is incapable of doing more than trimming bushes and mowing lawns."

Rae straightened and smiled bitterly. "Well, you just missed Mr. Waters, Junior, Burrows. He's got quite an idea about what to do with the garden."

"I have been expecting him, miss."

She stared at him. "You have?"

The butler nodded. "If I may say so, miss, Mr. Merriman was very foolish over the sale of his home. Naturally, young Mr. Waters would return to discuss the matter with him when all other avenues of communication have failed."

"Well, why didn't you tell Uncle Merry he was being foolish?"

The butler straightened to his full height. He wasn't very tall, but to the uninitiated, Burrows somehow always managed to project intimidation in spite of his size. "It wasn't my place to do so, miss."

Having been exposed to his imposing glare many

times, Rae just glared back. "It never stopped you from lecturing him before over something stupid."

"If you will remember, miss, my concerns were always for Mr. Merriman's personal excesses, not his business ones, but if I may say so, he's made very few."

"Well, this one was a doozy." She gripped the shovel handle tightly. "He agreed to sell the estate to Atlantic, then he came to me and told me what an idiot he'd been about the whole thing and that he was completely out of the deal. Next he told me he deeded over the place to me because he wanted to go into seclusion with what's-his-face—"

"Sri Patel."

"Thank you, Burrows. He wanted to go into the monastery with Sri Patel, because the Buddhist monk rescued him from bandits years ago, and they had had great philosophical discussions. Uncle Merry isn't even a Buddhist!"

"Episcopalian, although he wasn't a practicing member of the church," Burrows commented.

"Then," she went on, intent on venting her disgust with her favorite relative, "he gave me a song and dance about how he knows I love the 'old place,' and that I'll take good care of it. *Annnd*" —she pointed a finger at the stoic butler—"that it would be in better hands with me, than with him, because I wouldn't have even considered allowing it to be desecrated for condos. I fell for his line of bull like the righteous sucker I was. But Atlantic never accepted the down payment back, Burrows! He never told me that! And now I'm stuck fighting Atlantic." And Jed, she thought.

"Mr. Merriman has always avoided confrontation, miss."

"I'd like to confront him on the seat of his pants," she muttered, jamming the shovel into the mud. "Why didn't he just come to me in the first place, if he wanted to go live in a monastery and discuss philosophy with his old friend? Why did he have to make a deal with a land development company? And where the heck were his lawyers during all this?"

"I believe he felt you were quite happy with your life in New York, and wouldn't be interested in the estate—"

"Well, he was wrong," she broke in. "New York was only a convenient base for my business."

Burrows nodded in understanding. He ought to, she thought. The first thing she'd done upon moving in yesterday was to hook up her computer. That and a telephone modem were all she needed for monitoring the investments she made for her clients. She already felt more at home here than she ever had in her Manhattan townhouse.

"Mr. Merriman insisted on handling the sale of the estate himself rather than relying on his lawyers. His professional specialty was real estate law," he said in answer to her third question.

"Which he never actually practiced, thank goodness!" Rae said, realizing nobody would ever be able to answer the question of why Uncle Merry had gone to a land development company—except Uncle Merry. She hoped the razor slipped when the monks gave her uncle the traditional head-shaving. "But now I know how he managed this mess without anyone finding out until it was too late. Do you suppose he did something illegal?" she worried aloud, thinking of Jed's assurance that the estate couldn't have been legally deeded over to her with the agreement of sale still outstanding.

"It would not have served Mr. Merriman's purpose to leave you without legal recourse, Miss Rachel," Burrows said. "I suspect, though, that he did operate in a gray area of the law in order to deed the estate over to you. Something that would be open to several interpretations. However, if I may say so, miss, as a last resort you could probably have Mr. Merriman declared mentally incompe—"

"Burrows!" she gasped in shock. "I could never do that. Uncle Merry's crazy, but he's not senile."

The butler smiled the tiniest of smiles. "I didn't doubt you for moment, Miss Rachel."

She blinked. "Thank you, Burrows." A thought occurred to her. "Why did you let him go halfway around the world without you? You always traveled with him before, and now Uncle Merry's nearly eighty—"

She was interrupted by the dogs, who, having completed their mission, now raced into the herb garden.

"Get out of the damn mud!" she ordered Samson, as he leaped around her, happily trying to lick her face. The dog slunk away at the reprimand. Rae sighed and sat down on the edge of the hole. "Come here, you big goof."

She was knocked down by one hundred pounds of happy Great Dane. Although she playfully fended him off, Samson still managed to get in a few kisses. Finally, she gasped, "Enough already! Up!"

Once Samson had backed off, she sat up. Delilah, more dignified, settled next to her. Rae put an arm around the dog and tugged affectionately on its ears.

"What will you do now, miss?" Burrows asked in a grave voice.

Knowing he wasn't talking about the broken water line, she sighed. "Whatever I have to do to keep the estate from being turned into a marina-condominium complex."

An image of Jed standing in the maze flashed through her mind, and she shivered. As a child she'd loved him, and after he'd gone to college, she always thought of him with affection. He had been a friend, but now she felt as if she didn't know him anymore. He'd grown into a man—an attractive man. She pushed the thought away. Jed was right about one thing, though. What was for her a remembered and beloved refuge of freedom was just a piece of property to him. He'd probably been sent by the company because he knew Uncle Merry personally. She couldn't blame him for doing his job. Anyway, it would teach Uncle Merry a lesson if Atlantic leveled their legal cannons at him. All she asked was that they not set their sights on her too. Atlantic would be damn sorry if they did, she thought. Realizing who her opponent at Atlantic would probably be, she swallowed heavily. Uncle Merry's escape route was looking better and better by the moment.

"Do the Buddhists have nunneries, Burrows?" she asked.

"I believe so, miss."

"Good. Call one of them and get me a standing reservation, would you?"

By some miracle, the plumber actually arrived a short time later and began the process of replacing the split water line. After a needed shower, Rae was just wrapping a large terry towel around her when the telephone rang.

Knowing Burrows was still out "supervising" the plumber, she stepped over to the bathroom telephone and picked up the receiver. Her uncle had insisted on a phone in every room—even the bathrooms—not for convenience, but because he hated to hear them ring more than three times.

"Barkeley residence," she said briskly into the mouthpiece.

"Rae? It's Jed."

She clutched the towel more tightly against her damp breasts in unconscious reflex.

"What a surprise," she said in a soft voice that belied the tension building inside her.

"How's the broken water line?"

"Drier than I am," she muttered, then blushed when she realized what she'd said. "What do you want?"

"I need to talk to you about the estate—"

"I'm afraid you've got the wrong number, Jed," she interrupted. "You meant to call Uncle Merry's lawyers."

She hung up the phone.

It rang again.

Snatching up the receiver, she said angrily, "I told you—"

"Have dinner with me tonight."

Stunned by the unexpected invitation, Rae dropped the receiver and the towel at the same time. Falling to her knees, she scrambled to pick up both of them.

"What did you say?" she asked breathlessly, as she tucked the receiver between her shoulder and ear. She rewrapped her towel around her bare torso, her fingers fumbling with the ends.

He chuckled at her question. "Have dinner with me tonight. We'll just talk about old times, and how crazy your uncle is—"

Her laugh interrupted him. "You're a smooth talker, Jed Waters. But I have enough sense to know that the conversation would eventually wind up with a discussion of the estate, which I am not about to discuss with you."

"And which I don't intend to discuss with you. Not tonight. This is an invitation to have a nice quiet dinner with an old acquaintance."

"I would have preferred a nice quiet dinner with an old *friend*," she said sadly, and replaced the receiver on the hook.

The telephone didn't ring a third time.

Three

Jed sent flowers instead.

Cradling the bouquet of roses in her numb embrace, Rae stared at the card: "For Morticia Addams. With love from an old friend." The word friend was underlined.

With a laugh, she shook her head. Under any other circumstances, she would have been touched by the gesture. She looked up at Burrows, who was just shutting the front door after the delivery man.

"Flowers. How nice," she said in a wry tone. "And from Jed."

"If you will allow me, miss," Burrows said, taking the roses out of her hands. "I'll see to them."

"Thank you." Rae smiled. "But don't bother with a vase, Burrows. Just put them in the trash."

The butler merely raised an eyebrow at her odd request. "Shall I dip them in battery acid to hasten their demise?"

"Nice touch."

* * *

Seated across the desk from his boss, Jed gazed steadily at Henry Morrison's reddening face.

"He . . . he's gone?" Henry finally sputtered, his face turning an alarming shade of burgundy. "Barkeley's up and gone to a damn monastery?"

"I did warn you, Henry, that Merriman was a little . . . eccentric," Jed said, fully expecting the president of Atlantic Developers to explode like an overinflated balloon.

He wasn't disappointed. With a great bellow, Morrison slammed his hands on the gleaming cherry desktop. The roars continued unabated, though mostly incoherent to the human ear. The man's paunch actually seemed to shrink as he gave vent to a long tirade.

Silent, Jed waited out the tantrum. He'd given his boss bad news on more than one occasion, and the result had always been the same—an angry outburst, followed by cool logic. It all depended on how long it took Henry to run out of curses and breath.

Merriman had thrown everybody, Jed thought, and Rae had thrown him. Images of her, dirty face and all, had run through his mind as he drove back to the office. She'd grown up. Between the dogs and Merriman, he hadn't realized how much of an impact she'd had on him. The moment he issued the dinner invitation, though, he knew it was the wrong thing to do. They were on opposite sides of the problem with the estate. For the moment anyway, he acknowledged, as he reminded himself of his conversation with the company's legal department. He hoped she'd accepted the roses as the apology they were meant to be. It had been a long time since anyone had pricked his conscience, but Rae had done it with one word.

He refocused his attention on his boss, whose tantrum was beginning to wind down. Surreptitiously, he glanced at his watch. Four and a half minutes. Not too bad for Henry, he decided. If he was extremely lucky, he'd be able to pull off this next part.

"Call Legal!" Henry ordered, his voice still on a shouting level.

"I already have," Jed said calmly. "While there's been a breach of contract on Barkeley's part, our lawyers say the most we can get is our down payment back plus compensation, as we hadn't made settlement on the property yet. Barkeley was still the owner, and by law, he could deed the place away. Since he already showed good faith by attempting to return the down payment, the lawyers think they can reach a settlement without going to court."

"I don't want the damn money! I want the land!"

"How do you think I feel?" Jed asked in a disgusted tone. "I was the one who negotiated the sale in the first place, so I was hoping we could still sue for the estate."

His boss looked startled by the words, then nodded. "You put in a lot of hard work on this, I know. What about the . . . what did you say? Niece?"

"Grandniece." Jed mentally crossed his fingers

and plunged ahead. "Rachel Barkeley. I spoke with her briefly, and—"

"Well, talk to her again. Up the offer."

"Henry," Jed said in a soft yet very commanding voice. "The Barkeleys are old money. More money isn't going to mean a thing to Rae. It didn't to Merriman. He wouldn't have cared if we'd offered one-fourth the amount we did."

"Well, why the hell didn't you tell me that?"

Jed grinned. "Because Merriman deserved a fair price for the estate, and I still got him to agree to less than you expected to pay."

Henry chuckled.

"The company should get a good settlement from him," Jed said, cutting through his employer's amusement. "I talked to his lawyers, too, and they're so mad that he left them in the dark that they'll probably be on our side in this." Wanting to be able to answer any and all of Henry's questions, Jed had thoroughly checked on everything before approaching his boss with the bad news. "They want us to give them a figure and then they'll send somebody over to have Merriman sign the papers. It will take a while, though." Jed couldn't help laughing. "The way I figure it, right about now Merriman's hiking up a mountainside."

Henry's eyes widened in shock. "At his age?"

Jed nodded. "His lawyer told me that every year Merriman sends a donation of clothes and canned goods to a Buddhist monastery in Nepal near the Tibetan border."

"Tibet!" Henry exclaimed, shaking his balding head in disbelief.

"A church probably wouldn't take him," Jed

went on, with a straight face. "The head monk at this monastery is an old friend of his. Anyway, the last leg of the trip is by backpack and it takes a full week."

"He must be something," Henry said.

"He is," Jed agreed. So was his niece. "I'll have our cost figures ready by this afternoon, so a settlement—"

"I've already decided what to ask," Henry interrupted him, and named a figure.

Jed's jaw dropped in astonishment at the huge amount. "But that's—"

"Just about what our revenues would have been from the completed complex." Henry's eyes gleamed with anticipation. "It's a fair compensation to ask for damages. And as I have a board of directors to appease, I consider it more than justified. However, I don't expect to get that much. In fact, I don't expect to get it at all from that source."

Sensing what was coming next, Jed frantically tried to say something to block it, but he wasn't fast enough.

"Go back and talk to the niece. I'm sure she has a price."

Jed began his protest. "Henry—"

"I sense a reluctance in you, Jed," Henry said, leaning back in his chair and steepling his fingers across his belly. "I hope I'm wrong."

Jed stared across the desk at the older man. It was one thing to buy from a willing seller, but quite another to do what Henry was suggesting. "I'm reluctant only because I think we'd waste less time looking for a new site for the complex.

Granted, the Barkeley location was the most desirable, but there were a few others."

"Not as choice, and more costly."

"But available."

Henry made no comment.

"All right," Jed said, deciding on another tactic.
It was a wild gamble, but if it came off, everybody
would be happy. Including himself. He stood up.
"I'll talk to the niece on one condition."

"Name it."

"If I find you another site for the complex, just
as 'choice' and at the same price you were originally willing to pay, you drop the Barkeley estate.
All of it, including any litigation."

"And if you don't?"

"Then you have my head on a platter."

As soon as the words were out of his mouth,
Jed couldn't believe he had said them.

"It's your head," Henry said.

Jed gave him a curt nod of acknowledgement.
He wondered how happy his conscience would be
when it was standing in the unemployment line
with the rest of him.

Deftly avoiding the Brazilian consul's fancy foot-
work, Rae smiled politely as he whirled her across
the Warwick Hotel's elegant ballroom. She murmured apologies when her partner bumped her
into several other couples on the marble dance
floor. It was easy to read the Fred Astaire gleam in
Senhor Carreres's eyes, and she sighed inwardly.
She knew that if she weren't careful, "Ginger's"
toes would be squashed bananas.

Gazing around the gaily decorated ballroom, she decided her mother had really outdone herself in organizing the Ruby Ball. An annual charity event for UNICEF, it was one of the few Rae came back to Philadelphia to attend. In keeping with the ball's theme, everyone was dressed in various shades of red. Her scarlet chiffon gown was strapless, and the bodice, which was covered with twinkling sequins, was little more than a band around her breasts. The skirt was high-waisted and loosely gathered so that it flowed to her ankles. She had eschewed more elaborate jewelry for pearl-stud earrings and a matching tear-shaped pendant. Her hair was done in a simple pageboy that just brushed her bare shoulders.

From the din of cheerful voices that almost drowned out the small orchestra, she knew everyone was having a great time. Except her.

She admitted there was no reason why she shouldn't—barring Senhor Carreres's attempts to buff her toenails with the bottoms of his shoes. After all, she'd generously donated to a worthy cause, done her familial duty, and caught up with some old friends. And as she specialized in investments for wealthy women who had never actually handled money, a society function was always an opportunity for her to garner new business.

She refused to admit that it was one "old friend" who was bothering her. Still, she had expected to hear *something* from Jed in the last two days, especially after Uncle Merry's lawyers had assured her that Atlantic Developers had no claim beyond breach of contract. Unconsciously she winced, as she remembered how she'd impulsively run to the trash to retrieve the roses, only to discover that Burrows had taken her quite literally. The flowers were unsalvageable.

"Eess something wrong?" asked the consul, breaking into her thoughts.

Rae smiled and shook her head. The waltz ended in a flourish. So did Senhor Carreres, as he bent her backward over his arm. Once she was upright again, she pushed her hair off her face, stifled a sigh of relief and said, "Thank you for the dance, senhor."

"But it eess a medley, senhorita! Of the Beatles!" Mr. Carreres protested, as the orchestra immediately swung into the next number.

Before she could utter a lame excuse, someone came up behind her and said, "I beg your pardon for stealing Rae away from you, sir, but this is our song."

In shock, she twisted around as she was expertly taken into Jed's arms and whisked away from the surprised senhor. She'd never seen Jed in evening clothes, and he looked more than ever like a handsome stranger. Mechanically, she followed his smooth lead for a few turns, before she finally found her voice. "This is *our* song?"

He grinned at her. "Sure is. By the way, what is it?"

She giggled mirthfully. "*She Came In Through The Bathroom Window* by the Beatles."

"Ah. Didn't recognize the band's rendition, but I knew it in my heart, Rae."

She burst into laughter at his sincere tone. Still grinning, he pulled her closer and swirled her around to the music. Her momentary amusement

faded as she became aware of his hand, warm
and strong, against the small of her back, and
how easily her steps meshed with his. She realized she'd been unconsciously clutching the black
silk of his tuxedo, and she could feel the hard
muscles of his shoulder through the snugly-fitting
material. Her other hand was clasped tightly in
his. Somehow she couldn't force her gaze away
from his hazel eyes. He seemed to be looking at
her as if seeing her for the first time. A pulsing
began in her belly and spread outward at an alarming rate. This is crazy, she told herself, deliberately relaxing the hand on his shoulder. There
was nothing she could do about the other sensation, short of turning into a mannequin.

"What are you doing here, Jed?" she asked in
as formal a voice as she could muster, attempting
to dispel his effect on her.

"I'm dancing," he said matter-of-factly. "Why are
all the women dressed in red gowns?"

"It's traditional to wear red to the ball," she said
automatically, while deciding his mustache made
him look devilishly wicked. She shook her head to
try and clear it. "Why are—"

"So that explains all the red. At first, I thought
I'd wandered into a . . ." He grinned at her. His
gaze drifted downward, and she found herself
nearly quaking as he focused on her strapless
gown, scalding her bare flesh. Even though she
knew he couldn't see further, she was grateful for
the yards of flowing chiffon that kept the rest of
her hidden. "You look beautiful, Rae."

He drew her fully against him. His hard chest
pressed into her breasts, his strong fingers stroked

up her sensitive spine, his hips brushed rhythmi-
cally against hers for long hypnotizing moments.
She found she couldn't have pulled away, even if
she'd wanted to. It was only a dance, she rea-
soned. One little dance.

Jed attempted to ignore the innocent torture
she was perpetrating on his body, but it was as if
he were being enfolded in the gossamer wings of a
delightful angel. He had only wanted to see her
again—just once, and without the estate between
them—and the Ruby Ball seemed like a perfect
opportunity. He read about it in the morning paper, and noticed that her mother was listed as the
ball's organizer. It was a sure bet that Rae would
attend, so he called a few people he knew and got
himself a last-minute invitation. He had to talk
himself into dragging his old, rarely worn tux out
of the back of the closet. It was a tight fit—almost
too tight—and he felt a like a trussed-up turkey in
the hellish thing. But if wearing it to the ball
meant he'd have a good chance to repair some of
the damage to his relationship with Rae, he admitted he'd gladly suffer through one evening. To
actually have her pliant in his arms was like wishing for paradise and getting it. A tight tux was a
small price to pay for paradise, he decided. Not
questioning his good fortune any further, he
smoothed his right hand down her back in a
tender gesture . . .

At least he tried to. Frowning slightly as something pulled at his wrist, he glanced over her
shoulder to discover that his cuff link was caught
on the sequins that adorned her bodice. Damn
tux, he thought. His steps unconsciously slowed,

as he gave a gentle tug, trying to disengage his wrist. Nothing happened. Afraid of ripping the dress, he tried wiggling his wrist to get it loose. He didn't want to draw attention to them by using his other hand to maneuver the cuff link free. After all, they weren't at a high school prom, where the kids danced all wrapped up in each other.

"Jed, what are you doing?" Rae asked.

"I'm stuck on you."

"You're what?"

"My damn cuff link's tangled in your dress." He lifted his hand away to demonstrate his point, and her dress gaped open, exposing even more of the dreamy flesh of her back.

"Don't do that!" she exclaimed, reaching around and pushing her dress back into place.

"You're no fun," he complained, as she cut off his gorgeous view.

"This is not fun, Jed Waters. I feel like I'm about to be caught with my dress down!" Her fingers groped blindly behind her in an attempt to find the problem.

"Let me," he said, nudging her hand away with his forearm. "It's caught on the sequins."

Nodding, she replaced her hand on his shoulder. He tugged downward this time in an effort to get free. The back of her dress plunged dangerously low.

"Jed!" she yelped, then lowered her voice almost to a hiss. "This is not a backless dress, but it's going to be a frontless dress if you do that again."

"Think of it as a 'peekaboo' dress," he said, a huge grin on his face as the image of Rae's dress falling to her ankles flashed across his brain.

"I know," she grumbled. "One peek and you say, 'Boo.'"

"I'd never boo," he assured her, twisting his wrist around.

"Jed! Quit fooling around back there and get us free!"

"It's not easy when I'm doing it no-handed." He tried rubbing his wrist up and down to free his cuff link.

Rae made a desperate grab for her bodice, as the front slipped again. She barely managed to grasp the edge of it before her nipples were exposed, at the same time pressing herself as hard as she could against him to prevent an accidental peep show. She decided there was only one good thing about their present predicament. It had effectively killed her mind-drugging reaction to him. A hot flush heated her skin, as she realized how she'd given herself up to the dance. Forcing the thought from her mind, she acknowledged the dress was an acceptable embarrassment, compared to making a fool of herself over Jed. Finally, she said, "We've got to get loose somehow."

"Obviously, I can't do it this way without ripping the dress," he said. "Let's get off the dance floor. Then you can turn around and I can use my other hand."

She glanced around and spotted an alcove trimmed with velvet curtains. It didn't look too deep, but the curtains would give them a measure of privacy. She'd need some, just in case her dress decided to take a sudden trip to the floor. "That alcove—"

"I see it. Be ready for the fifty-yard dash—"

"Are you having a nice time, dear?"

Rae shuddered in horror at the familiar voice. Pressing even further against Jed, she barely turned her head to acknowledge her pretty, dark-haired mother, who was beaming at her in pleasure. Vivian Barkeley was dancing with an older man who looked very familiar.

"We're having a great time, Mom," she said in a rush. She nodded to her mother's partner, who smiled back. "Hello, sir. Well, see you—"

"But aren't you going to introduce me to your friend, Rachel?" Her mother beamed a second smile to Jed.

Rae made a strangled sound in her throat, before saying, "Jed Waters, meet my mother. Mom, Jed."

"You're even more beautiful than your daughter, Mrs. Barkeley," Jed said with a charming smile.

"What a lovely thing to say!" Vivian exclaimed happily. She indicated her dancing partner and added, "Have you met the Vice President yet, Mr. Waters? He's our guest of honor tonight."

With a quiet moan, Rae dropped her forehead on Jed's shoulder, as her mother introduced Jed to the Vice President of the United States. Her dress was going to fall off any second now, and her mother was making introductions. That was the trouble with good breeding, she thought in disgust. A person always had to make introductions.

She groaned aloud when Jed, with great aplomb, stuck out his right hand like a flipper to shake hands with the distinguished gentleman, and said,

"I'm sorry, Mr. Vice President, but I'm very attached to Rae at the moment."

"Now isn't that nice, Rachel!" her mother exclaimed, as the men shook hands. The Vice President, evidently seeing the reason for Jed's attachment, only chuckled.

"Wonderful, Mom. Just wonderful," Rae muttered, wondering how she could strangle Jed in front of hundreds of people and get away with it. Instead, she did a fair imitation of a Vulcan nerve pinch.

"It was a pleasure meeting both of you," Jed said, obviously getting the message, as he steered them between two other couples.

"Enjoy yourselves!" her mother called out.

"Nice guy," Jed commented. "Too bad I didn't vote for him."

Rae clenched her jaw in frustration. "Forget the Vice President, Jed, and just get me off the dance floor before the music stops!"

They danced rapidly toward the alcove. She was sure they'd make it, until she realized that the orchestra was signaling the last flourish of their grand finale to the Beatles medley. The last note died away when they were still a good twenty feet from their goal.

"We won't make it!" she wailed, bracing herself to grab the bodice the moment Jed let go of her.

"Sure we will," Jed replied, and proceeded to loudly hum the verse again as he danced her the rest of the way into the alcove. Once inside, Jed backed her into the corner next to the opening, and they collapsed against the wall. She immediately grabbed the front of her dress with both hands and yanked upward.

"Safe at last," Jed drawled, giving her a wry grin.

Relief washed through her, and she started to giggle. Remembering the glimpse she'd had of several startled faces as they passed by, she broke into laughter. She didn't know which was funnier, the headlong dash into the alcove like a couple of mad Beatles fans, or the fact that Jed couldn't carry a tune. His humming had been completely off key.

"You'd be a smash as a singer," she finally gasped in between chuckles.

"You ought to hear my *Rubber Ducky*," Jed admitted, grinning at her.

"Please," she said, as she turned her back to him. "I couldn't take it. Now let's get me unstuck."

With one hand free now, Jed worked the cuff link loose. She turned around to face him. A sigh almost escaped her lips, but the breath caught in her throat, as she found herself trapped by Jed's nearness. She glanced up at him and instantly felt an electrifying charge jolt through her. The alcove seemed to tilt at a wild angle, and she mentally tried to force it back into place. But she couldn't. His gaze grew hot, and color grazed his cheekbones.

"Jed," she whispered.

His mouth covered hers.

Four

Jed felt as if he were drowning. His blood thrummed heavily, vibrantly through his veins. Her lips were incredibly soft, and her response was a sizzling invitation to further delights. Rae whimpered in the back of her throat, as if in protest. Then her tongue mated urgently with his in feminine challenge and surrender. His control snapped.

He crushed her to him. His fingers sank into the tender roundness of her derriere, and he pressed her hips into his at the demand of his rapidly hardening body. Her arms were tight around his shoulders, her body a perfect fit. And her mouth . . . it teased and tortured, promising unique fulfillment. Like a man too long in the desert, he drank of her sweetness, trying to draw her into himself with just the kiss. Yet he craved more. No other woman had ever provoked such a response in him. She was incomparable, he thought. Her fragile exterior hid a core of steel and passion. A man could spend years peeling away the layers of Rachel Barkeley, and still not find her essence.

Abruptly the kiss broke off. Shocked and bewildered, Jed stared at her as she backed up against the wall. It occurred to him that all his memories of Rae were from long ago, and that's what had made the ferocity of the kiss so shocking. Then, she'd been like a pesky little . . . sister. But she wasn't little any more, and she'd never been his sister. The expression on her beautiful features reflected the same shock and bewilderment. The kiss had obviously taken her by surprise as much as it had him.

"Rae?"

"Great seeing you again. Hope you enjoy the ball," she mumbled, as she adjusted her bodice in an unnecessary gesture. She pushed aside the alcove curtain. "Good-bye, Jed."

He realized that she actually meant to leave, and he reached out and grabbed her arm to stop her. When she faced him again, he couldn't think of a thing to say. Her body was stiff, and he let go of her arm. She didn't move away. In desperation, he finally said, "About the estate . . ."

Immediately, the flustered Rae was gone, and he knew the mention of the estate had been a mistake.

"What about the estate?" she asked in a cool voice.

"It's not important," he said, shrugging his shoulders in dismissal.

She raised her eyebrows. "Now, why don't I believe that?"

Jed sighed. It was his own fault for bringing up the subject. He decided he might as well have put a sign on his back that said 'Kick Me.' "It really wasn't important, Rae. Just that there's no dispute of ownership. The estate's yours."

"Nice of your company to accept that little fact," she murmured, and stepped back into the ballroom. "But I expected to hear that from you days ago."

She turned and walked briskly away. Jed stepped out of the alcove and hurried after her. Taking her arm again, he walked along with her. She didn't pull away. "You really ought to hang around sometime and finish a discussion, Rae. We hadn't even gotten to the kiss yet."

She stumbled, then quickly recovered. "It was only a kiss. Men and women kiss all the time. Happens every day."

"If you think that was *only* a kiss, then you haven't been kissed nearly enough," he said, grinning at her. "Don't worry, though, I'm sure we can remedy the situation."

"I've been kissed plenty of times!" she exclaimed in outrage, as her cheeks flushed with color. She drew a visible breath in an obvious attempt to hold her temper. "Forget the kiss—"

"No way, lady."

"Jed!" She waved a hand. "What is your company going to do for a site now?"

Trying to find the right words, he hesitated for a long moment. "I've been authorized to look for a new one."

She stopped and he was forced to stop with her. Turning, she stared at him for an equally long moment, before asking, "And what happens if you don't?"

Barely aware of the crush of people passing by, he could almost feel a deep chasm opening between them. "Rae, let it go. For tonight, just let it go."

Her green-gray eyes reflected first confusion at his words, then understanding, then hurt. "You'll be coming back to me, if you don't find another site for your condos, won't you? Nothing I said made a difference. You still want the estate."

"The company does." Jed willed his gaze to stay on hers. "I've been busting my backside for the last two days, trying to find a new site for the complex. I had no problems with Merriman. He was willing to sell. You're not. If I don't find a site, I have no option but to come back to you. I told you once before that it was the perfect place for the complex, and my boss still feels that way."

"It's that damn deep water," she muttered, the disgust obvious in her voice. "The way everybody acts, you'd think the place was the fountain of youth or something. Well, bring on your high-pressure sales tactics, Jed Waters. But I'm not selling!"

She started to walk away again, and he pulled her back. "Oh, no, you don't. I get the last word this time, Rachel Barkeley. I had to do some fast talking to get Atlantic to agree to look for another site. Right now, I'm the best thing you've got going for you. Whatever happens, you remember that. And once the business is over, you better get ready for the real fight, so remember this."

Ignoring the gasps of the people closest to them,

he pulled her against him and planted a thorough kiss on her surprised lips. Finally, he let her go.

He hid a grin of satisfaction as he walked away.

Shaken, it took Rae several precious seconds before she could get her brain in gear. She realized she'd never before been so caught up in a kiss. Two kisses. And from Jed. Then his words sank in, and a thrill of joy shot through her. He was actually on her side over the estate! He was fighting to protect her interests as much as possible from his own company. It was a miracle turnabout . . .

Wait a darn minute, Rachel Barkeley, and think, she sternly told herself. Jed had snuck onto the estate in an obvious attempt to persuade Uncle Merry to change his mind about the sale. Not exactly the act of a forthright businessman. Now, two days later, Jed had turned into Mr. Nice Guy, just because *she* wasn't a willing seller? And the company had supposedly all but knuckled under, because they had no legal claim beyond breach of contract? Yet if the estate was the most desirable site, the logical course of action would be to press her to sell. Instead, Jed told her that was the last thing he wanted to do. Unless it was a reverse tactic . . .

"Why, that son-of-a . . ."

She clamped her jaw shut on the rest of the curse. She couldn't think of a better way for him to get her on his side than to pretend he was on hers. It was more difficult to say "no," when someone was being understanding and sympathetic—

even over something that meant a great deal to that person. Obviously, Jed still wanted the estate for his company, only this time he was going about getting it in a much more subtle manner. If he was "busting his butt" to find another site, then she was a monk! Talk about slick operators, she thought angrily. Used-car salesmen could take lessons from Jed Waters.

Lifting her gown slightly off the floor so she wouldn't trip over the hem, she hurried after him, determined to give him a piece of her mind. But when she spotted him heading for the exit to the lobby, she realized that venting her anger would be useless. He'd only dismiss her conclusions as farcical. She had no proof, just instinct—a good strong instinct that she was being softened for the kill. Still, it might be interesting to let him think that, she acknowledged with an inward grin.

When she was finally beside him, she looped her arm through his. Not stopping, he glanced at her, desire latent in his hazel eyes. A more primitive thrill shot through her this time, reminding her of their kiss. She realized that it probably hadn't meant anything to him. Her hurt stiffened her spine. "Jed, I want you to know how much I . . . appreciate what you've told me." She hid the sour taste in her mouth under a smile. "You realize, though, that I'm now forewarned."

"I just wanted you to know that the estate is business," he said. "It's my job, and although I don't have to like it, I will do it."

"I understand that." She paused for a moment, trying to find the right words to show proper sympathy. "I probably understand your position more than most people would. After all, with my family's banking interests, I've been hearing about how businesses work since before I could walk."

"Good," he said, his steps slowing. A slow smile broke out on his face. "Could I interest you in a cup of coffee? It'd be a change from the lemonade we used to drink."

Rae hesitated. Tempting as his offer was, she decided a momentary retreat was safer. The ball was almost over anyway. "Much as I'd love to, I have to be going."

To her surprise, he only nodded and said, "Let me walk you out to your car."

"I have to get my cape," she said, as relief and an odd disappointment washed through her.

As they walked in silence toward the cloakroom, she decided her disappointment was due to the change in Jed. The Jed she remembered had had integrity. No matter how distasteful the job his father had delegated, Jed had always done it well and without an adolescent complaint. She wondered what had happened in the intervening years to twist him so.

Her thoughts were interrupted when she reached the cloakroom. She retrieved her black wool cape from the attendant. Jed took it from her and wrapped it around her shoulders. Touching his mustache, he asked, "How badly would I blow this truce, if I suggested we have dinner together tomorrow night?"

He wasn't wasting any time, she thought with disgust. She had enough sense to know that some companies would do almost anything to get the land they wanted, and Atlantic Developers was a very powerful conglomerate. Much as she wanted to avoid the headaches Atlantic could cause her, she admitted it was better to face the problem head on. That meant dealing with Jed. Taking a deep breath, she said, "I think the truce would hold up."

At his almost boyish grin, Rae sighed inwardly. She felt as if she'd just agreed to go three rounds with Muhammad Ali. If only she could load her glove with iron horseshoes.

"Eight o'clock?"

"Fine, fine," she said, as she racked her brain for some solid ammunition. An anvil wouldn't hurt. She barely noticed when he tucked her hand in the crook of his elbow and began leading her out of the ballroom.

Jed was right in one respect, she decided. As Atlantic's representative, he had a good deal of input into the company about the estate. If he recommended that the company should make a real effort to find another site, it probably would. Now if only she *could* get him on her side. If only he could see the estate as more than a viable piece of property . . .

"Got everything?" he asked, then added, "Your purse. You don't have your purse."

"I never bring one," she said, as his words captured her attention. She patted the cape at waist level. "Those little evening bags are ridiculous, and I wind up having to hold the thing all the time. Instead, I keep what I need in a hidden pocket." She chuckled. "Now that I've let out my secret, I'll probably get mugged."

"Or else you'll be taking the dogs everywhere you go," he said, smiling wryly.

Rae made a face at him. "They try that anyway."

As they walked toward the lobby exit, she admitted getting him to fall in love with the estate was really a silly idea. She had been forgetting that, for all the time he'd spent around the estate as a boy, he had no personal attachment to it. Still, Jed's opinion *had* to be a deciding factor with Atlantic. He had handled the transaction with Uncle Merry, and he was still in charge of acquiring property for the marina complex.

"Rae? Are you married?"

Startled, she glanced up at him. He was grinning at her.

"I thought that would get your attention," he said. "Now that we've established that you're not married—"

"We have?"

"Sure. No wild-eyed husband punched me out for that kiss."

She refused to answer that, and instead said, "What about you, Jed? Are you married?"

He shook his head. "I almost was. It was right before I graduated from Villanova. One day the girl said, "I found the cutest house for us, and the patio is a great place for my sorority to meet.""

"Oh, Lordy," Rae muttered, as a vision of a pink-cashmere-clad cheerleader ran through her mind.

He grinned. "After that, I made it a practice to leave her alone with my college roommate as much as possible. He could afford the patio."

She giggled. "You are a stinker, Jed."

"Yeah. I tell myself that every year at their anniversary party. On the patio."

Laughing, she shook her head. They reached the hotel's revolving doors.

"Any entanglements?" he asked, squeezing next to her and pushing the door around to the outside.

"Once, almost. Like you," she said, remembering. "It was the oddest thing. We were having a before-dinner drink at his place, and I went into the bathroom. He'd left the shower door open, and there was a damp shower cap hanging over the shower head. His initials were monogrammed on the cap. I kept staring all evening at his perfectly groomed hair, and giggling."

"He . . . he . . ." Jed burst into laughter, as they emerged into the chill night air.

"I know. It seems like a dumb reason not to get married. But the truth is, the shower cap just made me realize how many other things were wrong. It never would have worked. After that, there always seemed to be a shower cap or something else wrong with my dates. Overly cautious, I guess."

The doorman, having seen the preceding party to their car, now approached Rae and Jed. Tipping his hat, he said, "Miss Barkeley. Did you enjoy the ball?"

"Yes, thank you, Bill." She smiled at him, while reaching into the hidden pocket inside her cape. She pulled out a slim wallet and handed him a generous tip. "I hope the car wasn't too much trouble."

The doorman tipped his hat to her again, then

pressed a set of keys into her hand. He glanced over his shoulder to the antique Rolls-Royce parked to the right of the hotel entrance. "No trouble at all." He leaned forward and lowered his voice. "I told the police the Rolls was part of a display for the hotel."

Rae grinned, as Jed turned and stared at her in astonishment. "That's your car?"

"Uncle Merry's, actually," she admitted. "Surely you remember it. He's had it for as long as I can remember."

"Vaguely." He grabbed her hand and pulled her toward the car. "Teenage boys, Rae, are only interested in flashy new cars to impress girls. Men, though, have a more discerning eye for the machine itself."

"I'll try to remember that," she said, smothering a laugh at his haste.

"Beautiful," he murmured, when they halted in front of the car. He gently touched a finger to the gleaming shadow-gray finish on the front fender. "Just beautiful. I wanted to look at her earlier, when I first got here, but she was drawing quite a crowd."

"It's a '56 Phantom," Rae said, as Jed squatted down to examine the shining chrome of the spoked wheels. "I probably shouldn't have taken it out, but I just couldn't resist. I'll be relieved, though, to get it home in one piece."

"Merriman once offered me a ride in it," Jed said in a far-off voice. "And I was stupid enough to hold out for that Maserati he had."

"It's still sitting in the garage. He liked his cars, didn't he?"

"Mmmmm." Jed rose to his feet and walked around the car, admiring it.

Rae grinned. Obviously, Jed liked cars too. At least, he was having a love affair with the Rolls. "Want a ride?" she asked, when he rejoined her on the sidewalk.

"Now?"

"Think of it as an early Christmas present." She unlocked the passenger door. "Hop in."

He grinned back at her, and she felt as if she *had* just given him a present. She decided there might be something in having him on her side— even if she had to give him the Rolls to get him there.

It would take more than a car, she dryly reminded herself, shutting the passenger door. She walked around the front of the car to the driver's side, unlocked it, and slipped into the tan leather seat. Jed sighed audibly when she started the ignition, and the car purred to life. She pulled it away from the curb without a jolt.

"I must have been nuts."

"What?" she asked, concentrating on the Center City traffic.

"To hold out for the sports car. I must have been nuts."

She chuckled. "Did you ever get a ride in the Maserati?"

"Once. But it wasn't like this." Out of the corner of her eye, she saw him caress the wood paneling on the dash. "This is like ice cream on a hot day. Smooth, rich, and satisfying."

"Oh, brother, are you hooked!"

"It doesn't take much, when you're around something like this," he said, with a sheepish chuckle.

At his admission, all her earlier thoughts came back to her in a rush. Jed on her side . . . his word having weight with the company . . . getting the man to fall in love with the house . . .

Rae's eyes widened in shock. Maybe it wasn't such a crazy idea, after all. Put the man in the house and let him fall in love with it. It might work. What the hell, she thought, he was already in love with the car. Coming to an instant decision, she swung the car around a corner and floored the gas pedal. The Rolls shot forward like an arrow from a bow—clean and fast.

"Rae!" Jed yelped in astonishment. "Are you crazy?"

"Runs in the family, Jed," she said, swerving around the other cars in the street. "It gets worse during a full moon. Check and see if there's a full moon, would you?"

"Slow down, or we'll have an accident!"

"Oh, I hope not," she said with a nervous giggle. "It would ruin the kidnapping."

"What!"

She let go of the wheel with one hand and patted his knee. "I'm kidnapping you, Jed. So sit back and enjoy the ride."

Five

"You're kidnapping me!" Jed exclaimed, positive he hadn't heard her correctly. "This is a joke, right?"

"You can laugh after the ransom is paid," she said as the Rolls screeched around another corner. "Besides, what's a little kidnapping between friends?"

Although unconvinced about her seriousness, he realized the car was heading farther and farther away from the hotel—and at a rate of speed that was unsafe for the traffic. She was certainly going all out to pull off the punchline, he thought. Deciding to take her advice, he deliberately relaxed back against the leather seat cushion.

"I don't mind being kidnapped, Rae," he said in a casual tone, playing along with her. "But I would like to get to the hideout in one piece. Could you slow down a little?"

"As long as you promise not to jump out of the car at the first stoplight."

"And miss my kidnapping? Heaven forbid!"

She immediately slowed the Rolls to a more normal speed, and they rode in silence. It wasn't until she steered the car onto the ramp of the Benjamin Franklin Bridge that he began to wonder if she really was kidnapping him. Amused by the thought, he admitted he couldn't think of a more beautiful kidnapper than Rae. The only question he had was why she would do it. It certainly wasn't for the money. He chuckled to himself. It would be interesting to see what she intended to do with him once she got him to her "hideout." He leaned his head against the back of the passenger seat and closed his eyes, thoroughly content to go along for the ride.

Half an hour later, Rae brought the Rolls to a stop in front of the portico of her new home. She glanced over at Jed, who hadn't uttered a word since he'd asked her to slow down. His eyes were closed, his chin rested on his chest, and his body was slouched down in the seat. It was depressing to realize her kidnappee had fallen asleep.

"Wake up, Jed!" she snapped, disgusted with him and herself. Hell, she thought, her first kidnapping, and the victim had slept through most of it! She shut off the engine and yanked the key out of the ignition.

"Where are we?" he asked, rubbing his eyes as he sat up.

"At the hideout. Come on." Getting out of the car, she spotted Burrows opening the front door. The foyer light silhouetted his figure in the entry.

She slammed the car door shut and hurried up to him.

"Good evening, miss," said the butler. "Did you enjoy the ball?"

"It was . . . different," she replied. "By the way, I've kidnapped Mr. Waters. He's in the car."

"Very good, Miss," Burrows said without hesitation. "Shall I put him in the cellar? I believe that is standard practice among kidnappers."

"I think we can find better accommodations for him." Annoyed that Burrows hadn't even flinched at the news, she wondered if she'd skipped something important, like fireworks at the scene of the abduction. Still, very little fazed Burrows, she admitted. He was an old-school butler. "Put Jed in the trophy room. He'll be company for Harvey." She smiled in satisfaction at the thought.

"I doubt that Mr. Waters will be happy sharing a room with a tarantula."

"Why not? Harvey won't eat him." Harvey had been a gift from Uncle Merry to his great-grand-nephews, her brother's children. Her sister-in-law wouldn't allow the spider in her house, so Harvey stayed at the estate. Rae suppressed a shiver, realizing for the first time that she'd been deeded custody of the pet along with everything else. She wasn't exactly crazy about Harvey either, but the boys loved him. The inner tension that had given her the stamina to get home now drained out of her, and she suddenly felt tired and apathetic. Hearing the passenger car door open, she acknowledged that she just didn't have the energy to face her kidnappee. "I'll leave Jed to you, Burrows. I'm going to bed."

As she stepped into the warmth of the house, she vowed that the next time she kidnapped someone she'd bring Harvey along as an accomplice. A tarantula was sure to liven things up.

The next morning, Rae sat in the breakfast nook in the kitchen and stared at the cup of coffee cradled in her hands. Before she turned in last night, Burrows had tapped on her door and informed her that Jed had settled into the trophy room with very little complaint. She had yet to see him this morning. Thank heaven for that, she thought, unconsciously hunching her shoulders in shame.

The same thoughts she'd had during her restless night returned, and she wondered where the hell her common sense had been the night before. How could she have even seriously considered kidnapping Jed? What if he had her arrested? She shuddered at the thought, knowing that the crime was a felony. What had possessed her to do it?

She would be facing him at any moment, and she had no idea how to explain her insane actions. She never would have conceived of the kidnapping, if he had truly been a stranger. That was the problem, she decided. She kept forgetting herself with him. Maybe her best bet would be to apologize for any inconvenience, and hope he would think it was all a joke.

Grasping at the idea, she bolted upright in her chair. That was it! Just treat the whole mess as a joke. He'd probably be annoyed with her, but he surely wouldn't think of going any further than that.

Hearing footsteps, she glanced sharply at the doorway then slumped in relief as Burrows strode into the room.

"I believe our 'prisoner' will be downstairs shortly," he said, as he moved to the ten-burner range. On its own island in the middle of the work area, the range was the focal point of the kitchen. Burrows lifted a copper pan down from among the cookware hanging over the stove. "Might I suggest mulberry pancakes, miss."

"No thanks," she mumbled, her stomach flipping at the thought of food. "I'm not hungry. Jed would probably like some, though."

"I believe, miss, that haute cuisine is unacceptable fare for a kidnap victim. I have taken the liberty of preparing bread and water for Mr. Waters. You, however, must eat something more substantial."

"Burrows!" she gasped. "I did not kidnap Jed—"

"Could have fooled me," Jed said, coming into the kitchen.

Rae whipped around to face him. He had on the pants and shirt from his tuxedo. The silk sleeves were rolled up to expose the corded muscles of his forearms. His hazel eyes were gleaming with amusement, and the grin under his mustache was positively rakish. He took the seat to the right of her. Inhaling the clean sharp scent of him, she swallowed back a wave of butterflies. "Jed. I was just kidding last night about kidnapping you. It was only a joke, and—"

She interrupted herself as Burrows set a plate with several slices of bread on it and a glass of water in front of Jed. "Your repast, sir."

Jed glanced up at the butler. "You've got to be kidding, Burrows. How can Rae return me in good condition if I don't eat properly?"

"I'm sorry, sir. I hadn't realized. Of course, if your stay with us is to be a short one . . ."

Burrows' voice trailed off, and both men turned questioningly to Rae. Jed asked, "How long will it take to get the ransom money? By the way, who are you going to ask for the ransom?"

She groaned aloud. "I'm not asking anybody!"

"Then I'll be around for a while." Jed picked up the plate and glass and handed them back to Burrows. "Eggs over easy and bacon, please. And coffee."

"Would you care for some mulberry pancakes, sir?" Burrows asked. "I have the batter already prepared."

"Great!"

Rae groaned again.

"Very good, sir." Burrows returned to the range.

Turning to her, Jed rubbed his hands together in anticipation. "Now that breakfast is settled, we've got to figure out who you're going to get the ransom from. Like most companies, Atlantic has a policy of not paying ransom money for their employees, so they're out."

"Jed—"

"My parents are retired now, so their income is limited," he continued. "My brother just graduated from med school, so he doesn't have a thriving practice yet. Gee, I'm beginning to feel like the kid in the O. Henry story who nobody wanted back."

"Dammit, Jed!" she exclaimed, waving a hand

in the air. "The kidnapping was just a joke, okay? After breakfast is over, I'll drive you back to the hotel so you can get your car."

"You were very serious last night, weaving in and out of traffic like the entire Philly police force was after us," he pointed out. "Why would you bring me here otherwise? Or lock me up with a tarantula as a guard?"

"Well, I . . . uhm . . . see . . ." Humiliated at her own sputtering, she lamely said, "You can go now."

"But I can't," he protested. "I've got to stay here until a ransom is paid. That's Article Four, Section One of the Kidnap Handbook. By the way, Harvey is a good guy to bunk with. He doesn't snore."

"Cute, Jed," she snapped. "But you're not staying. You are supposed to be looking for a new site for the complex, and you can't very well do that if you're kidnapped, can you?"

He stroked his mustache for a moment, then said, "As long as I have a phone to keep in touch with my people, I can, and it'd be a damn good way for you to make sure I do. What's the matter, Rae, are you chickening out?"

She glared at him. "There's nothing to chicken out of!"

"Then I'll just hang around until we can figure out who's going to pay the ransom. I assume I have freedom to move around the house and grounds. After all, you can always set the dogs after me. Where are they?"

"Outside," Burrows said, before she could give a caustic reply. He set a cup of coffee in front of Jed. "Your breakfast will be ready in just a few minutes, sir."

"Thanks." Jed glanced down at his lap. "I'll need a change of clothes, and my car is still at the hotel. If they haven't already towed it away. Have you had it moved, Rae? It's a dead giveaway that I'm missing."

"Damn you, Jed," she muttered through gritted teeth.

"After I have finished here, I can retrieve your car for you, sir," Burrows volunteered, returning to the work area. He expertly flipped the eggs over in the pan. "Mr. Coe, our next-door neighbor, owns a bookstore in Center City. He can drive me in. Miss Rachel really shouldn't return to the scene of her crime."

"Burrows!"

"Excellent," Jed said, grinning at the butler. "Could you stop by my place and get me some clothes?"

"I believe I could, sir."

Furious with the two of them for teasing her, Rae jumped to her feet. "That is enough! If it makes you so damn happy, Jed, then consider yourself kidnapped." She shook her finger at him. "But you damn well better be on that phone, really trying to find a new site for the complex. And you damn well better find one!"

She whirled on her heel and stalked out of the room.

After breakfast, Jed eventually found her in the music room. He assumed it was the music room, since a grand piano sat in regal majesty in one corner, a harp reposed in another, and gleaming white shelves held stacks of sheet music.

He stood in the doorway and watched her as she sat motionless on a chesterfield sofa and gazed out the French doors to the terrace. Her chin was thrust out in stubbornness, and her eyes were wide and unfocused. Her slender body was relaxed, yet there was an inner tension about her. Lord, she was beautiful, he thought. Outwardly cool and elegant, but inside all fire that ignited a man until he burned out of control.

With a silent chuckle, he remembered his shock of the night before when he realized she was actually serious about kidnapping him. He still couldn't quite believe that he had been shut up in a huge room full of stuffed game animals and one live spider in a glass aquarium. The only other pieces of furniture had been two sets of bunk beds. Burrows told him the game animals were the victims of Merriman's hunting days and the bunks were for Rae's nephews who occasionally stayed overnight. Jed grinned, thinking that thousands of boys would have traded their Rambo toys for a night in that room. Likewise, he wouldn't trade a night in the trophy room for a month at the Warwick—unless, of course, Rae was with him.

Sobering, he wondered if Rae's initial anger had cooled, or if it was still boiling. Maybe he shouldn't have waited until after breakfast to go looking for her. At the time, though, it had seemed better to let her be alone for a while. She had to accept that he was staying put. A man would be a fool to walk away from such a beautiful and intriguing kidnapper.

She turned suddenly to face him. Immediately, he smiled and walked into the room. "Burrows is leaving to get the car. Any last-minute instructions?"

"I can think of several," she said in a dry tone. "None of them repeatable in mixed company."

"I should be the one to be angry, Rae," he said, taking a seat next to her on the sofa. He made no comment when she adjusted her body none too subtly away from his. Instead he added, "I was the one who was kidnapped, not you. And I'm going to stay kidnapped."

She frowned at him. "You're not behaving like a proper kidnap victim, Jed."

"I must have skipped the etiquette chapter in the Kidnap Handbook," he replied.

"No kidding. Well, since you insist on staying, you are now considered a guest." She made a face. "You might as well be, after the breakfast you had. You may come and go as you please, and the sooner you please to go will suit me fine. I feel like I just let the enemy into the general's tent."

"Rae, you can't change the game plan halfway through the first quarter," Jed said, not sure he liked being thought of as a guest. As a kidnappee, there would be all sorts of possibilities to be negotiated. But as a guest, the rules for good manners were already laid out. The last thing he wanted to be with her was on his best behavior.

She gave him a sugary smile. "Jed, I am the kidnapper, and as such I am the one who decides how the victim will be treated. I firmly believe my victims should be given all the comforts of home, with as little intrusion on my part as possible. I'm sure you'll find everything you could possibly want or need." She rose to her feet. "Oh, and feel free to use the phone. For anything."

He reached out and pulled her down onto his lap. He grinned as she squirmed to free herself from his tight embrace. "Keep that up, and I know the first thing I'm going to require."

She froze, but there was an angry green fire in her eyes. "Why do I have the feeling you're going to be as hard to get rid of as 'Red Chief'?"

"Why do you keep trying to walk away in the middle of a discussion?" he asked in return. "The Rae I remember couldn't stop talking. I'd be clipping hedges, and you'd be right beside me jabbering away about anything and everything."

"Maybe I'm all talked out," she said, arching an eyebrow.

"Maybe you're lonely," he countered, gazing around the room. Ten people could have lived in it, he thought, and never touched each other once. "Was that why you hung around so much whenever I was working here? You were lonely?"

"*I* was being friendly!" she exclaimed indignantly. "And believe me, Jed, you looked like you needed a friend."

"More than likely," he admitted. "I was one of those moody teenagers. You grew up on an estate like this one, didn't you?"

She frowned at him. "I did a lot of growing up here, Jed."

"So you did." He wondered what it was like to grow up with such wealth and luxury. His parents had had a comfortable house in a development, where the homes came in only three styles and the streets were named after the fifty states and their capitals. True suburbia, and worlds away from her, he acknowledged. Or maybe not. Despite their differing backgrounds, they'd both been lonely children.

"Could I get up now?" she asked, breaking into his musings.

He gazed into her eyes for a long moment. "No."

His sudden kiss took her by surprise. His mouth was warm and coaxing, and Rae found herself responding to it just as she had the night before. His arms were around her, safe and comforting, and she forgot everything—the estate, her anger, his slick ways. Her lips parted at his tongue's tender invasion, and a languid heat started deep inside her belly and spread outward along her veins. She wound her arms around his neck, plowing her hands through his thick hair. She moaned into his mouth as his palm cradled her breast, and his demanding fingers brought it to a hard aching peak. Clutching at him, she moaned again in supplication. The kiss turned white-hot, and she dimly realized that she wanted more and was terrified, all at the same time.

The want and fear fought each other for a brief instant, but before the outcome could be resolved Jed gently broke the kiss.

"I don't think I want to get ransomed," he murmured.

In spite of the panic she felt roiling inside, a giggle escaped her. Deep down, though, she knew she was in trouble. She shouldn't be enjoying his company. Worse, she shouldn't be so attracted to him. This time when she tried to get up, he let her go. She headed for temporary refuge by the piano. Somehow, she had to put even more space between them, and telling herself over and over how his every move was designed to get her to sell her home didn't seem to help. She needed something more.

A feeling of excitement mixed with dread washed over her, as she watched him rise from the sofa and come toward her. She told her feet to move, but a sensual anticipation kept her traitorous body rooted to the spot. No man had ever affected her like this, she thought wildly.

When he stopped in front of her, she finally found her voice. "I'd better find Burrows and get him to pick up a few things while he's out."

"Coward," he said softly, as she slipped by him and hurried toward the door.

"With a big yellow stripe down my back," she muttered to herself, her feet racing even faster across the Brussels carpet. In the safety of the hallway she decided that after she found Burrows, she'd call the dogs inside. She would need all the help she could get to stay away from Jed. Then she'd call her brother and borrow her nephews for the weekend.

It was definitely time for a meeting of the Barkeley Club.

Six

"You heard right, Ross. I'm staying at the Barkeley estate."

Jed chuckled into the telephone as his acquisitions manager excitedly shot questions at him. He finally broke through the rapid-fire quizzing. "You'd never believe me if I told you, so I won't bother. Listen, Ross, I'm sorry to be calling on a Saturday, but there are a few things I want you to do for me before Monday."

"Go ahead."

Jed knew the man was still brimming with curiosity, and he appreciated that Ross didn't pursue the subject. Leaning back against the kitchen counter, he said, "I need copies sent here of all the Delaware River property preliminary reports. Also the cost effectiveness grids Janine worked up for them."

"Okay, but you know we've gone over and over them this past week."

"I know. Send them anyway, and send the phone numbers of the realtors we deal with in Maryland, Virginia, and D.C. I want everybody aggressively looking for a new site, Ross. Make sure they understand that. I don't know when I'll be back at the office, but if you need to reach me call me here." As he gave Ross Rae's telephone number, he heard a rhythmic ticking sound behind him. He glanced over his shoulder to see Rae's monstrous dogs trotting into the kitchen, their nails clicking against the tile floor. "I've got to go, Ross. Oh, and tell Henry I'm checking out a site in . . . Harrisburg."

"Harrisburg? Henry won't like it."

Jed grinned as the animals sat down several feet away from him and stared. "How I wish Henry were here right now."

"What?"

"Never mind. Talk to you later, Ross." He hung up the phone and turned to face the Great Danes. He smiled. "Hi, guys."

The dogs just stared. They were going to be a problem, Jed decided, if they didn't stop their guardian angel act. Somehow he would have to make friends with them. Somehow . . .

Spying a possible solution, he took two steps to his left. The Danes didn't move. Taking a deep breath, he casually sauntered to the refrigerator and said, "I bet you two are hungry."

Opening the refrigerator door, he searched until he found a small brick of cheese. He pulled it out and removed the plastic covering. Holding it up, he grinned at the animals whose eyes now ignored him for the food. "How about some cheese?

Nice delicious cheese for . . ." He racked his brain to remember the dogs' names. They were named something biblical . . . Adam and Eve? He chuckled, finally remembering. "Samson and Delilah."

Both dogs perked up their ears, but the one on the right craned its neck forward, its black nose testing the air. Jed tossed the cheese to it. The dog caught the brick in midflight and wolfed it down, then looked up in anticipation.

"There's more where that came from," he assured the animal, then leaned sideways to check its sex. "Samson. More cheese, Samson? It beats the hell out of kibble."

The dog's tail wagged briskly in answer. Jed squatted in front of the open refrigerator and began rummaging around for more goodies. Suddenly he felt hot breath on his neck. He froze. Turning his head, he found Samson looming over his shoulder. The animal's cavernous jaws were open and a large pink tongue licked at gleaming teeth. Fortunately, the dog's eyes were trained on the brimming contents of the refrigerator.

"You're some guard dog," Jed murmured, pulling out a long package that he assumed contained deli meat. He opened it and smiled when he saw a hefty quantity of sliced corned beef. He proceeded to feed Samson two slices at a time, being careful to keep his fingers out of harm's way. Once the meat was gone, he decided it was now or never and held out his hand palm down. Wagging his tail happily, Samson licked Jed's hand. "You're a pussycat at heart, aren't you, pal?"

Finding a huge hambone in the back of the fridge, he gave it to Samson to gnaw on. He picked up another wedge of cheese and, rising to his feet, turned his attention to Delilah. The female still hadn't moved. He tossed her the cheese. It landed on the floor at her feet, and though she glanced down at it, she never touched it.

Jed sighed. "You are as stubborn as your beautiful owner."

Delilah growled in agreement.

He tried some leftover duck, more deli meats, even a hunk of lamb roast smothered in mint sauce. The dog never budged. Jed acknowledged that there was no sense risking his hand when she wouldn't even take his bribes from a distance. Samson, enticed by the varying smells, left his bone and wandered over. Delilah immediately snapped at her companion in warning and covered her growing pile of doggie delights with one paw. Jed cringed at the messy sight.

"What the hell is this?" Rae demanded, stepping into the kitchen.

"A get-acquainted party," Jed quipped, inwardly wincing at being caught trying to subvert her dogs.

Delilah yipped like a puppy, drawing her owner's attention. Jed wasn't sure whether the dog was asking permission to eat or ratting on him and Samson.

"Good Lord! That's expensive deli meat!" Rae exclaimed, running her hands through her hair. "And half a lamb roast! And the Stilton! Burrows is going to have a fit!" She turned to him, anger glowing hotly in her eyes. "Jed! How could you?"

"They looked hungry, Rae," he said innocently. Samson trotted back to him and nudged his hand, obviously hoping for more food. He absently caressed the dog's head.

Rae gaped in astonishment at them. "Samson, you traitor! Corner!"

At her command, the dog slunk away, his tail between his legs. Then, he slunk back and picked up the bone, before continuing to the nearest corner. Settling on his haunches, his back to his audience, the dog dropped the bone on the floor and stared at it. A wave of guilt overtook Jed at the dog's dejected look. He joined Samson in the corner, patted his massive head again in commiseration, then faced the wall too.

There was silence in the room. Finally, Jed heard low obviously reluctant chuckles behind him. He grinned.

"What are you doing?" Rae finally asked.

"I been bad, too, Ma," he drawled over his shoulder.

She erupted into laughter. Jed and his fellow convict turned together to watch her amusement. Samson, evidently taking it as a sign that he was off the hook, lay down on the floor and began working on the bone.

"Don't make me laugh, Jed," she said, as her mirth subsided.

"Why?" he asked, thrusting his hands into his pockets and leaning against the wall.

"Because I like you when you do."

She gazed at him for a fleeting second longer, and he felt as if she'd just let down an invisible barrier between them. Then the doorbell rang, and her expression instantly became guarded. The dogs raced for the door.

"You can clean up the mess," she said. Samson raced back into the kitchen and began to gobble down Delilah's cache. She smiled sweetly. "You can also clean up the mess he's going to make later, after he gets sick."

"Thanks," he muttered, as she left to answer the door.

Samson gave the now bare floor a final lick, then galloped after her. Jed followed at a slower pace, down a short wide hallway into the foyer. A grand curving staircase wound its way up and backward to a landing high above, and as he passed underneath it he couldn't help but admire it once again. If a prettily pouting Scarlett O'Hara were to suddenly come sweeping down, he wouldn't have been at all surprised. It was like stepping back in time, he admitted. The image of Rae, dressed in her red gown, gracefully descending the staircase ran through his mind. He grinned, thinking Scarlett would have run a poor second. His amusement faded as he wondered if strangers would care about the mansion's beauty and heritage as much as Rae did, if it were turned into a clubhouse. He doubted it. High piping voices reached his ears, breaking into his musings.

Jed rounded the staircase to find the front door wide open and three young boys racing after the dogs outside on the front lawn. Rae was talking animatedly to a older male version of herself, who was lifting suitcases from the back of a Mercedes. Rand Barkeley had been a less frequent visitor to the house, but Jed had met the good-looking, poised older brother on several occasions. As a teenager, Jed had always felt inadequate and awkward around Rand, and that old sense of insecurity rose within him again, making him reluctant to go outside and greet Rae's brother. He wished Burrows had returned with some decent clothes. His tuxedo trousers and shirt were hardly appropriate dress for morning and were sure to raise eyebrows. He had no wish to embarrass Rae.

Boys and dogs suddenly burst through the open door. They skidded to a halt in front of him. He noted that the two older boys were strikingly dark-haired and blue-eyed, while the younger was less dramatic in coloring, with medium brown hair and eyes. Delilah growled at him.

Jed grinned at the dog, admiring her determination. "Hi."

"Who are you?" asked the youngest.

Jed judged him to be about four or five years old. "Jed. Who are you?"

"Michael. I'm five."

"I'm thirty-five."

"That's old," said Michael.

Jed smiled. "Yeah, but I get to have a great big birthday cake"—he made a round circle with his arms—"to hold all the candles. And it gets bigger every year."

The young boy's eyes widened. "Wow!"

"I'm Mark," the middle boy said. "Are you the electrician?"

Jed blinked at the odd question. "No."

Mark's face fell. "Oh."

"An electrician almost blew himself up fixing our lights, and Mark missed it," volunteered the oldest. He thrust out his hand in an adult gesture of politeness. "I'm Randall Barkeley, sir."

Jed shook his hand, then in turn shook the other boys' hands. Each one had a disconcerting adult grip, as if they'd practiced many times—even young Michael. "I'm very pleased to meet all of you."

"There you are, Jed," Rae said, as she and her brother came into the house. "Rand, you remember Jed Waters."

"Of course," Rand said, offering his hand. "I envied the way you could do backflips so effortlessly. I damn near killed myself trying to imitate you."

Shocked and surprised, Jed nearly forgot to shake the man's hand. Quickly recovering, he took Rand's firm grip in his own and said, "I don't think I could do them now. It's been too many years. How are you?"

"Fine. How's your dad?"

"Fine," Jed said, again surprised that Rand would have even remembered his family. He realized he was still shaking hands and immediately let go.

"So Rae's kidnapped you," Rand said with a grin. He ignored his sister's gasp, and added, "She certainly makes life interesting."

Astonished that Rand seemed to be enjoying the idea of Rae as a kidnapper, Jed stared at him for a long moment, then grinned widely. He transferred his gaze to Rae's delicately flushed features and murmured, "I think she makes it more than interesting."

"Don't you have to go, Rand?" she asked in a caustic tone.

"Much as I wish I didn't, Alicia will be waiting." He grinned at his sons. "Okay, guys, you're off duty. Cram as much fun as you can into the weekend, but don't tear the house apart, and I'll pick you up tomorrow night."

Confused by Rand's odd words, Jed watched the boys grin back at their father in complete understanding. He realized there was only one enviable thing Rand Barkeley had now, family. Unconsciously, his gaze returned to Rae. Her arms were crossed over her chest, and she was looking at her nephews with a mixture of love and amusement.

Rand offered his hand again, saying, "Good to see you again, Jed."

"Same here."

After shaking hands, Rand added, "And good luck. I believe Rae intends to use the boys as new and unsurpassed torture."

Jed laughed.

"What's unsurplussed?" asked Michael.

"Unsurpassed," Rae corrected, ruffling his hair. "That's you, sweetie."

Rand smiled. "Good-bye, guys, Jed." His voice went up two octaves and he added, "Good-bye, Auntie Rae."

She made a face at him.

The door had no sooner closed after their father than the boys erupted with a thousand questions and comments. Jed chuckled, as Rae waved a hand to silence them.

"First things first. We'll go upstairs and unpack and see Harvey. And please don't let him out of his cage." The boys groaned. "Burrows says it took him three days to find him the last time. Michael, you can sit on Samson later!"

"Did you really kidnap that man, Aunt Rae?" Mark, the middle boy, asked.

"Yes. Now upstairs."

"Wow!"

Admiring the curving outline of her jean-clad derriere as she followed the boys up the staircase, Jed smiled to himself. He could still feel her lips on his. Her mouth had been so soft and incredibly sweet in surrender. She'd admitted she liked him—and he knew she didn't want to. Her emotional defenses were weakening, and so were his. His career was in the balance, and yet he was more worried about pleasing Rae than his company. Unfortunately, there had been no opportunity so far to really talk to her, and it looked like there wouldn't be until after her nephews left tomorrow evening. He wondered what would have happened if the boys' visit had been delayed another week . . .

If Rand's words were correct, then the boys' arrival had been a last minute plan by Rae. His smile widened when he realized she was using them as a form of physical protection. But who didn't she trust? Him?

Or herself?

"And this is a front door too."

Rae sighed in exasperation as Michael, her youngest nephew, grinned happily up at his new friend. Closing the door in question after all of them had passed through, Jed smiled indulgently at the child.

"I know," he said, transferring his smile to her. "A long time ago people used to sail on the river, so everyone had their front doors put in backwards so they could watch out for pirates. Then everyone got smart and started using the road, so they put in a second front door. But," his voice lowered dramatically, "on a dark and stormy night you can still hear the pirate ghosts howl as they search the river in vain for ships to loot."

As the boys chattered excitedly about pirates and gold, Rae hid a smile. She hadn't been much older than Michael when she'd proudly told the same story to Jed. Years later, she'd been disappointed to learn that the pirates had been part of Uncle Merry's imagination.

"Beat ya to the river!" Mark suddenly yelled.

The older boys and Samson immediately broke into a run across the patio and down the sloping lawn. Little Michael's chin quivered as he stopped and watched.

"They run too fast."

Jed scooped him up in a fireman's hold, saying, "We may still lose, buddy, but we'll have fun doing it!"

Michael's high-pitched giggles reached Rae's ears as Jed dashed after the rest of the group. She looked down at Delilah, who continued at her mistress's slower pace, and said, "He found Samson's weakness for people food, and now he's got a friend for life. Michael thinks he's the best thing since ice cream. Mark thinks his being kidnapped is great. Randall discovered he likes Harvey, and Burrows treats him like a treasured guest. Even my brother likes him, because he could do backflips. You're the only decent judge of character in this family, Delilah."

She wished she could say the same for herself, but she too had fallen under Jed's spell. It was his standing in the corner with Samson that had done it, she decided. She liked him. In spite of everything, she liked him. And the longer he stayed, the stronger her feelings toward him would grow. The thought terrified her.

She admitted it was her own fault. Until she'd kidnapped him, she'd been relatively safe. Her emotions had been firmly in control, and she'd been able to keep a tight rein on her attraction to him. But there had been a fire in that first kiss, a fire she hadn't known she was capable of feeling. What would happen when that fire finally went out of control?

Allowing her question to go unanswered, she inhaled the cool crisp air and made her way down to the riverbank. The back gardens were fading with the promise of winter but were still beautiful, and the trees were in their autumn glory. At the edge of the property, the muddy blue river rolled past, its deep ripples endlessly joining, one after another. The estate had always seemed like an ageless sanctuary. No, not quite like a sanctuary, she corrected herself. It was like coming home. A Barkeley had built it, and a Barkeley had sold it, and a Barkeley had bought it back again. A Barkeley would keep it this time, she vowed, while trailing a loving hand along a browning azalea bush.

Deep laughter captured her attention, and she looked up to see Jed pointing toward the river as he explained something to the boys. His lean body was outlined in the jeans and blue hooded sweatshirt he'd changed into after Burrows had returned from his errands. A drugging warmth flowed through her body, and she hugged her arms around her middle in an attempt to fight the sensation. Even as a child, she'd been drawn to him. What she was suffering now, however, was a purely adult reaction. She wanted him. Knowing she wanted the wrong man didn't stop the feeling. In fact, it only made the warmth burn hotter and deeper. While the boys' presence would keep her physically safe from Jed, she realized they were no barrier against what was happening inside her. That was something only she could fight.

Joining them at the steep riverbank, she forced herself to relax. Delilah finally raced off with Samson on a doggie hunt, and, with a sense of resignation, Rae watched her go. Delilah might not have accepted Jed yet, but the dog obviously realized everybody else had. Including herself.

She sat down next to Michael at the top of the stairs that led down to the wooden dock and said, "Did you win?"

"Almost," her youngest nephew replied, satisfaction in his voice. "Jed runs real fast."

"And Jed's pooped out," Jed added, sitting on the grass next to the steps. He casually leaned back on his elbows.

Rae was all too aware of the hand that rested only inches away from her hip. She swallowed and fought the urge to lean back against him.

"Do you think the pirates took their prisoners over there and tortured them?" Mark asked, pointing to the woods directly across the river.

"Bloodthirsty brat," Rae said affectionately, reaching over Jed's middle and cuffing her nephew's leg. Mark grinned at her.

"Maybe they hid their treasure there," Randall commented, staring at the tree-lined horizon.

"Maybe they did," she said, getting to her feet. "And it's up to the Barkeley Club to find out. Everyone to the car!"

The boys whooped. Grabbing Michael's hand, she started running for the garage on the far side of the house. Suddenly, Jed was running on the other side of Michael.

"Can a Waters join the treasure hunt?" he asked.

"Yes, please!" Michael gasped and took his hand too. His feet stumbled as he tried to keep up with the adults. The older boys passed them.

As one, Rae and Jed lifted the little boy off his feet. Michael screamed with fear and delight as he literally flew through the air.

"Almost makes you wish you were five again," Jed said, grinning at her over Michael's head.

Rae had no breath to answer. Silently, though, she admitted she'd never want to be five again.

It was much too young for what she was feeling.

Seven

"Coffee, sir."

Startled by the interruption, Jed glanced up from his reading to see Burrows entering the drawing room. The butler carried a heavily loaded silver serving tray.

"Thanks, Burrows," he said, rubbing his tired eyes. "Where is everybody?"

"The young gentlemen and Miss Rachel have turned in for the night." Burrows set the tray down on the low Duncan Phyfe table in front of the sofa. Lifting a silver coffeepot, he poured the steaming black liquid into a delicately flowered porcelain cup. "If I may say so, sir, you should turn in too. The hour is late, and young boys are no doubt quite enthusiastic on a treasure hunt."

"So my bones tell me. What an afternoon! But I'm almost finished here." In spite of his disappointment that Rae had gone to bed, Jed smiled as the strong bitter aroma of hot coffee reached him.

"Will you be needing anything else, sir?"

"No, thanks." A question that had begun to intrude into his thoughts earlier surfaced again. "Burrows? You've been with Merriman for a long time, haven't you?"

The man stopped rearranging the sugar bowl and creamer and straightened. "Forty-three years, sir. I . . . entered his service during the war."

"The estate was his home for even longer than that, wasn't it? He told me he'd bought it in the thirties."

"That is correct, sir."

He looked around the large high-ceilinged room. The deeply polished wood peeping out from under a magnificent Persian carpet was probably the original flooring. Heavy sky-blue velvet curtains were pulled back from the tall narrow windows, and all the walls were wainscotted in glossy white paneling. The carved molding around the ceiling, fireplace, and doors was still intact and probably dated back to before the Revolutionary War. Even without the antique furnishings, the room was stunningly beautiful. He shook his head and asked, "Then why would he want to see it torn up for condos?"

"I couldn't say, sir."

Professional poker players showed more expression than Burrows did. His features stayed as formally blank as Jed had ever seen them. So much for trying to get an answer out of Burrows, he thought.

Once Burrows had left the room, Jed sipped his

coffee. It had a soothing aftertaste, and he realized there was an added warmth to the brew that spread down his throat and into his belly. He sipped again, trying to identify it. Whiskey! From its smoothness, he judged it was probably aged Irish whiskey. Leaning back on the plush sofa, he rolled a third sip around his tongue, letting the alcohol permeate his senses for a few moments. He swallowed and grinned, thinking that while the house symbolized wealth and elegance, Burrows made living in it luxurious. Managers of five-star hotels could have taken lessons from the man.

Sighing, he reached over and picked up the reports. Just after dinner, he'd taken over the room to read them yet again, hoping he'd find something to indicate a viable property elsewhere. He hadn't found one—not yet—but he had found a puzzling little fact. If the figures were correct for the various developed properties the company had looked at, then Merriman had agreed to sell for a good deal less than the estate was worth. Jed knew he'd negotiated a very good price for the estate, but he'd never realized before just how good. He remembered how eager Merriman had seemed about the deal—almost gleeful—and how he'd insisted on a fast sale. Jed knew what he'd told his boss, Henry, had been true: Merriman would have gone even lower. Merriman had always been eccentric, but nobody had ever called him foolish. He wondered if the old man had baited a hook in a calculated maneuver guaranteed to reel in Atlantic. But why? And if he just wanted to get rid of the place, why deed it over to Rae? He already had a buyer. There was no explanation for Merriman's crazy actions, Jed admitted, except his finally going " 'round the bend" and realizing it afterward.

Suddenly feeling more tired than before, he glanced down at his nearly empty cup and chuckled. Burrows certainly didn't fool around when he decided someone ought to be in bed. He began stacking the reports into a neat pile, deciding to take yet another look at them tomorrow. Still, he couldn't shake the feeling that everyone had somehow been suckered by a crazy old man.

After returning the coffee tray to the kitchen, he slowly climbed the back stairs to the second floor. He stopped in front of the room Burrows had told him was Rae's. The temptation to open the door and enter was overwhelming, but he steeled himself to continue down the hallway to the trophy room. He crept inside and discovered Michael had appropriated the bottom bunk he'd used the night before. The young boy was snuggled down under the quilt, sound asleep. He grinned at Mark and Randall who were sleeping in the two top bunks. Michael had probably lost the choice spots to his older brothers. After checking to make sure the tarantula hadn't been let loose, Jed stripped off his clothes and crawled into the last available bed beneath Randall.

Burrows was right, he thought. The boys had been enthusiastic about the treasure hunt, and he was exhausted. They'd dragged him all over that damn park in a wild haphazard search for gold and jewels, and Rae had been worse than her nephews. He managed a weary smile as he remembered how she'd climbed trees and pointed out likely spots for a pirates' trove. The boys obviously adored their aunt. So did he. She'd been like a sprite, full of imagination and mischief, and more than ever like the Rae he remembered. When they all returned to the car to come back home, he noticed a smudge of dirt on her cheek and that she'd broken three nails, but she didn't even seem to care. She'd hardly acted with the elegant coolness she'd shown the night before. Yet he found her even more beautiful. Her cheeks had been pink from the cool air, and her eyes shining with fun. It had taken an enormous amount of control to keep his distance from her all afternoon.

Once, though, he had seen her lose her joyful expression. They had penetrated the dense woods to the riverbank directly opposite the estate. He'd been admiring the peaceful picture the stately red brick mansion and its gracious surroundings made, when he'd turned to find Rae gazing at him with accusing eyes.

He knew now he was the one she didn't trust—not with her home or her feelings. Her defenses might drop for a moment, but they always snapped back into place. The estate lay between them, an unsurmountable barrier. So far, he'd only managed to temporarily circumvent Henry from launching an all-out campaign for the property. There were many ways to put pressure on a reluctant seller, and Rae would be subjected to all of them unless he found some way to appease Henry.

Trying to rid himself of his disturbing thoughts, he rolled over, immediately banging his knee into the wall. He smothered a curse at the too small bed, and tried to ignore the fact that there was a much larger, less lonely one down the hall. He doubted if it held the welcome he wanted. Still, the thought teased and tantalized him as he finally drifted off to sleep. . . .

He was in the middle of the park again, only it was covered with a frigid white mist. Naked, he ached from the cold as he trudged among the barely visible trees and bushes, his every movement causing him even more pain. He knew he was supposed to be looking for something, but he couldn't remember what it was. Then a little girl stood before him. She began to grow until she turned into the most beautiful woman he'd ever seen. She was wearing a garment that was a wisp of nothing, and her slender body moved with the grace of a goddess. A light breeze lifted her midnight hair from her shoulders, and her green-gray eyes promised him the love and comfort he'd been searching for. Clumsily, he moved forward and covered her mouth with his cold lips. Her soft flesh warmed his hands, and he touched her everywhere—breasts, belly, legs— until he found the heated core of her. The kiss turned hot with her passion, and her body writhed urgently against his. Blood pounded into his loins, driven by the sensual fire he knew only she could create. Suddenly, she vanished from his arms, and all the park's trees turned into condominiums, surrounding him in their horrible prison. He tried to break free, but everywhere he turned another concrete building hemmed him in. The woman reappeared, floating in the mist beyond his reach. He silently cried out to her. She was above him now, looking so sad. Then she bent her head toward him, her lips parting to bestow a kiss. A light seemed to issue from her. It was dim at first, then it became brighter and brighter. It blinded him, its heat burning his face. . . .

"Jedidiah Waters! You have been called!" intoned a deep voice.

"No condos!" he shouted, bolting upright in bed. Young voices giggled, and he opened his eyes in bewilderment. The terrible bright light was shining directly in his face! He slapped it away. There was a clunk and a thump, and the light was gone. Nightmare over, he slumped in relief.

"Master Randall, if you please," said the voice.

Confused that the voice hadn't gone away with the light, Jed looked around. He couldn't see a thing in the pitch black, but he heard someone moving about.

"Who is it? Who's there?" he asked sharply.

"I am afraid we have awakened the gentleman too abruptly," said the voice. "Terribly sorry, sir, but we must adhere to the ritual."

"What ritual?" He swallowed at a horrible thought. "Is this hell?"

The young voices giggled again. They sounded suspiciously familiar. Shaking off the last of his sleep, he realized the voices belonged to Rae's nephews. Huey, Dewey, and Louie, he thought furiously.

"Dammit, guys—"

The light was suddenly in his face again, and

the deep voice repeated, "Jedidiah Waters! You have been called!"

He blinked against the pain in his eyes. "Burrows? Is that you?"

"Yes, sir."

"What the hell are you doing?" he roared in outrage.

"Calling you to a meeting of the Barkeley Club, sir—"

"Geez, we thought you'd *never* go to sleep!"

"Master Mark!" Burrows said in reprimand. The direction of his voice shifted back to Jed. "You have been nominated, sir, and now you must answer the call."

"I'm not answering anything except sleep, and get that damn light out of my face!"

Suddenly the light was pointing toward the floor. Jed rubbed his eyes, trying to get rid of the spots spinning inside them.

"Please," Michael said, crawling into the bed next to him. "I nominated you to be in the club. You have to join."

Jed lowered his hands and looked at him—or tried to. All he saw was a small dark lump.

"Please," said Mark and Randall together.

"It is quite an honor Master Michael has bestowed on you, sir," Burrows added.

Jed sighed in defeat. Between the "call" and his nightmare, he'd had the sleep scared out of him anyway. Condos and Rae. He shuddered. "Okay. What do I have to do?"

The boys cheered, and Burrows thrust something into his hands. "Put on this robe and slippers, sir."

Getting out of bed, he fumbled around in an attempt to find the robe's opening, then realized it was styled like a monk's robe. Must be Merriman's, he thought while pulling it over his head. He pushed his feet into the open-backed slippers Burrows had thoughtfully provided. His eyesight finally adjusted, and in the flashlight's glow, he noted Burrows and the boys were dressed the same as he.

"I thought Halloween was still two weeks away," he said in amusement.

"So it is, sir. Please follow us."

"It's only a little scary," Michael said, taking his hand.

As he was led through the dark house, he decided that whatever the hell the Barkeley Club was, the meetings took place at a damned inconvenient time. His brain could barely function, and his body insisted he find the nearest bed and collapse onto it.

"Wait here, sir. Master Michael will return for you, when everything is ready," Burrows said, opening a door that was tucked under the arch of the back stairs. The narrow staircase faded downward into what seemed like a black hole.

"Right," Jed said in a flat voice.

He watched them eerily vanish one by one into the hole. He waited impatiently and was about to go back to bed, when Michael finally returned. Although the boy only motioned for him to follow, he saw that the youngster had a huge grin on his face. As he stumbled down the steep stairs and through the dank basement after his small friend, Jed decided he'd just walked into an Edgar Allan

Poe story—boys dressed in monks' robes, flitting through an old mansion in the wee hours of the night, vanishing staircases. It was either Poe, or a Scooby-Doo cartoon.

He realized they'd reached their goal when they came to the far end of the basement. It was lit with candles, and a single cane chair faced a long table that was covered with a red cloth. Randall, Mark, and Rae sat behind the table. She wore a white wool robe, its hood framing her fragile features. Surprised and yet not surprised, Jed stared at her. She was beautiful and regal in the soft candlelight, and his erotic dream came back in full force.

Burrows appeared from a darkened corner and banged a long staff on the concrete floor. "Sit and be judged worthy, Jedidiah Waters."

Jed grinned at the rare use of his given name and sat in the cane chair. He grinned even more widely at the lovely judge he faced.

"Michael Barkeley, present your evidence."

The little boy stepped in front of the table. "Jed . . . knows all about pirates . . . and he helped with the treasure hunt," Michael said hesitantly, then turned and looked unhappily at his nominee, obviously unable to think of anything else.

"You forgot that he's kidnapped," Mark whispered loudly.

"Oh, and he's kidnapped!"

"And he talks in his sleep!" Randall added in a low voice.

"And he talks in his sleep," Michael echoed.

Jed wondered frantically what the boys might have overheard. The dream had been very vivid.

"And he fed my Stilton cheese to the dogs." This contribution came from Burrows, who frowned at him.

"Yeah! He fed the cheese to the dogs, and Burrows didn't even spank him for it."

The butler loudly cleared his throat, and Jed turned his face away to keep from laughing.

"And he's my friend," Michael said proudly before lapsing into silence.

"All good reasons, Master Barkeley," Rae said, smiling at him. "But he must also pass the test of the Barkeleys. Lord Chamberlain, blindfold him."

"Yes, Grand Master."

Burrows produced a black scarf from his sleeve and tied it around Jed's eyes. He couldn't see through the silk, but he heard a lot of giggling and scuffling. Finally, warm feminine hands encircled one of his and guided it into a bowl containing something cool and squishy. He realized he was supposed to identify it. Fortunately, he'd played this as a kid and knew the answer.

"It's Jell-O."

The bowl was whisked away and another presented. He had no trouble with the spaghetti, mud, pine cone, and ice cream, although he felt as if he were back in his dream when his fingers ached from being thrust into the cold dessert. All the while Rae's hands covered his, her slender fingers almost caressing as they moved his hand into each bowl. Finally, his hand was wiped clean and turned palm upward. Something warm and sticky yet hairy, was placed into it. For the first time, he had no idea what it could be.

Then it began to move.

"It's Harvey," he said in a hoarse voice, willing himself not to flinch as two of the spider's legs began to inspect his thumb.

Harvey was gently lifted from his hand, and the blindfold finally removed. Michael ran over and hugged him.

"Well done, Mr. Waters," Burrows said. "I do believe that is the first time we have had a nominee guess every item correctly."

"Thanks," Jed muttered, still not recovered from the last item. He decided he liked Harvey best at a distance. He smothered a sigh of relief when he saw Randall put the tarantula into a small hamster cage and close the wire door.

Mark stared at the spider. "It mighta been neat if Harvey'd bit Jed."

Burrows rapped the staff on the floor several times. "Call to order! The nominee has passed the test, and now the Council will vote."

Michael ran behind the table and sat in an empty chair that Jed hadn't noticed before. Each of the boys voted approval, but when the Grand Master's vote was called for there was a momentary silence as she stared at the nominee.

"No."

The boys loudly protested their aunt's vote. Jed refused to admit he was hurt by Rae's rejection. It was only a child's game, after all. But, dammit! Why couldn't she have kept their differences out of it? Poor little Michael was nearly crying.

Burrows banged the staff again for silence. "I vote yes. A majority approval has been reached." The boys cheered. "The Grand Master will now give the Oath of Blood."

Reluctantly, Rae rose to her feet. She hadn't meant to vote against Jed joining, knowing the boys, especially Michael, would be disappointed in her if she did. The Barkeley Club was for them, after all. But something inside her had protested loudly against admitting him to the inner family circle.

She walked slowly around the table until she was in front of him. Jed stood up. She kept her eyes focused on his robe. She could see his broad chest rise and fall with each breath.

Burrows took her hand and pricked her forefinger with a needle. Blood welled up from the tiny cut. He did the same to Jed, then bound their fingers together with a piece of string. Surpressing a shiver, she felt as if the binding went far deeper than ceremony. She forced herself to continue with the initiation.

"Raise your right hand, Jedidiah." When he did, she said with a straight face, "A Barkeley will always believe in Santa Claus and the Easter Bunny. A Barkeley will like school and always eat his peas. A Barkeley will have fun at all times, but never at the expense of another. A Barkeley will be kind to his fellow human beings and deal fairly with them. A Barkeley will keep his body and mind fairly clean. Above all a Barkeley will uphold the honor of all the Barkeleys." Finally she looked up into Jed's face. Expecting to see amusement in his hazel eyes, she found their expression dead serious instead. Swallowing, she added, "To accept this oath is to accept the responsibilities that go with it."

He gave her a tiny half smile. "I accept."

"Then by my authority as Grand Master of the Barkeley Club, I now pronounce you a full member." The boys cheered as soon as she finished.

"Congratulations, sir," Burrows said, stepping forward to untie their fingers. "You are now a true Barkeley."

Rae shuddered at the thought.

After the basement lights had been turned on, Burrows shepherded the boys back to bed. Rae blew out the candles and began to gather them up. She tried to ignore Jed as he watched her.

"You lied to Michael, you know," he finally said, breaking the silence.

She had appeased her nephew's feelings by telling him she'd only wanted to add a little spice to the voting with her objection.

"I know."

"It's only a children's club, Rae."

She turned around to face him. "I used to think so, Jed. Just a little bit of scary secret fun in Uncle Merry's basement. It wasn't until I had to give you the oath that I realized I've never drifted far from the words. It bothered me somehow to let someone into our group who was never going to take the oath to heart. They're not bad words to live by."

He gazed at her for a moment, then held out his hand. "Come upstairs. I have something to show you."

The sincerity in his eyes made her come forward and take his hand. They walked through the basement and up the stairs in silence. The house was quiet, with only the foyer light on to guide their way.

Jed led her into the drawing room and switched on a lamp by the sofa.

"I've already seen the sofa," she said in a lame attempt at a joke.

"Sit down, Rae."

All too aware that she was alone with him, she sat on the edge at one end and toyed nervously with her robe.

He sat down next to her and picked up a pile of papers from the table. "These are the company reports of the various properties we looked at before we decided on the estate. I asked for them to see if we missed anything anywhere that would make one of them more attractive to the company as a site for the Condos. Instead I found something else. Do you know what Merriman's selling price was?"

She nodded.

"A little low, don't you think?"

"It seemed so to me," she said cautiously. "But real estate is cheaper here in Jersey."

"That's true." He flipped through several pages, then pointed to a line. "This is an old Port Authority warehouse down in Gloucester. We didn't go for it because of the refineries across the river. Not exactly a great view for luxury condos. Look at the price."

She bent over and carefully read the computer line detailing the size, location and price of the property. It wasn't very much less than the price of the estate, but it seemed to her quite a lot for an old warehouse. "It's overpriced, isn't it?"

"It's reasonable for a *commercial* property. Rezoning would have been another problem." He flipped the pages again. "This one is an abandoned restaurant with available acreage right on the Delaware Bay in the Villas."

She read the line and looked up at him. "It's nearly the same as Uncle Merry's, but that's commercial, too, right?"

"Residential properties can go for more down there. It's a summer resort town. Rezoning it wouldn't have been a problem, like the warehouse." He grinned at her. "Unfortunately, horseshoe crabs commit suicide by the hundreds on the bay's beaches, and the tide isn't strong enough to take them out to sea. Not all the towns along the bay bother with the expense of removing them, and the smell can be . . . unpleasant on a hot day."

"Ah."

He showed her several more properties, residential and commercial, and she began to see a pattern. Though the properties were priced lower, each had some undesirable element to them. "I understand now. Even though the estate is higher in price, it's still the best suited for your marina complex."

"No, that's not it. Not quite. The point is that these are all developed properties, though not kept up, and their market price is not much less than what Merriman agreed to sell for. Haven't you noticed all the housing construction that's been going on in south Jersey? It's true property in Jersey is still cheaper than in the surrounding areas, but when you're talking about a marina complex on the Delaware River, you're talking about a limited amount of viable property still left to build on. This place is akin to a czar's summer palace, and yet Merriman was ready to sell it for a fraction more than the others."

"He really must have wanted to get out," she said in a low voice.

"Did he? Remember, he'd never put it on the market. I came looking to buy, which was to his advantage."

"Now I don't understand."

He made a face. "I was hoping you wouldn't say that, Rae, because I don't understand it either."

She remembered what had originally caused him to show her the reports. "What does all this have to do with the club?"

He chuckled. "I've always liked to think that my parents took over for Santa and the Easter Bunny, rather than admit they didn't exist, and I always eat my peas. I've done things in my life that I haven't been proud of, but the deal for the estate isn't one of them, Rae. Merriman was very willing to sell, and it didn't take much to reach a price."

She leaned back against the cushions and closed her eyes. She believed him. It wasn't that she hadn't before, but she'd been able to place him in a villainous role. Now, though, she could see just how big a part her uncle had played by making the deal too good to pass up. He must have known what he was doing too. If she didn't know better, she'd swear he'd actually been trying to dump the estate on Atlantic Developers.

She felt Jed settle back on the couch next to her. Turning her head slightly toward him, she opened her eyes. It always surprised her in some way that he wasn't the young boy she remembered so well. Maybe it was the mustache, she thought.

He gently traced her cheek with his forefinger. "I'm not a knight in shining armor, but I'm trying to keep you safe, Rae."

"I think," she said slowly, "that I believe you, Jedidiah Waters."

Jed smiled. "It's a start."

Eight

The words swirled enticingly through Rae's mind. Maybe it was a start for both of them . . . an understanding. A heady warmth flooded her veins at the thought, and she smiled at him.

Jed muttered a soft curse, and lowered his head. His lips touched hers softly, almost hesitantly. They lifted, then dropped back again for another teasing caress, and another, and another, before his mouth settled upon hers and moved slowly. Her spine tingled. She knew she shouldn't allow him to kiss her. Jed's kisses were dangerous. And tempting. She savored the way their lips merged as if made for each other. His fingers curved around her jaw in a gentle grip, even as their tongues entwined in a languorous mating. She told herself she shouldn't be doing this. She really shouldn't. Things were complicated enough between them.

But it was just one little kiss. Just one, she silently promised herself. Just one.

She slid her palms up his chest to encircle his shoulders, her fingers finding the iron-hard muscles underneath his robe. His arm tightened around her, bringing with it a long-sought feeling of warmth and protection. Suddenly, he pulled her hard against him, and the kiss exploded in a white flame of desire. She groaned in the back of her throat, as the last of her resistance crumbled against the onslaught of his tender demands. Dimly, she realized that something inside her had been waiting—waiting for Jed, and now that something had surfaced, dragging her helplessly into the kiss. To push him away would be to push away an integral part of herself.

Her mouth twisted and turned in perfect response to his, and all the while she hungrily wanted more. Her fingers delighted in the feel of his hair, the strong column of his neck, the tensile strength of his back. His hands gently cradled her breasts, his fingers teasing her nipples into aching points through the robe. There was a roaring in her ears, and she clung to him, the torment inside her beyond anything she'd ever known before.

Jed felt as if he were back in his dream. No other woman had held the honeyed fire she possessed. It was what he had been searching for in the cold mists of the park. It was what he held in his arms now. The overwhelming want and need pounding through his body demanded the satisfaction of reality. Desperately, he buried his mouth in the hollow of her neck, tasting the satin flesh he'd always longed for. The unique scent that was Rachael Barkeley filled his senses. He'd waited a lifetime to claim her, he thought. He knew that now, and she would know it too.

He eased her back on the sofa, his body pressing hers deep into the cushions. He slid lower, his lips exploring every inch of her through the soft wool. Her nipples were diamond hard, and he suckled them. Her belly quivered under his mouth, and her thighs shifted restlessly, tantalizing him with her need. He resisted her hands as they clutched at him, trying to draw him back to her. Kneeling at her feet, he stroked her slender ankles, marveling at the fragile bones. He glanced up at her face. Passion flushed her cheeks, and her lips parted slightly as a low moan escaped her.

"Jed, please," she murmured in a husky voice.

"I want to know all of you," he whispered, his voice raspy.

Slowly, he slid the white robe up her body, exposing the slim calves, the lush thighs. He sucked in his breath at the sight of her white silk bikini panties, which barely veiled her shadowed femininity. The smooth curving line of her hips blended into a small waist, and his hands devoured the silken skin of her ribcage as he pushed the robe higher. Finally, he exposed her full, upthrust breasts and the coral-tipped nipples that were beckoning to him. The glory of her pulsed within his already rock-hard body, and his last remnant of control broke. Heat scalding his cheekbones, he fumbled as he tried to get the robe off her. Gentle hands helped him finish the task. He skinned off the panties, then yanked his own robe over his head. His briefs swiftly followed.

He lowered himself between her parted legs, the shock of his hot flesh meeting hers shuddering through him. He nuzzled first one breast, then the other, swirling his tongue around the velvet pebbles. She twisted feverishly under him, and he gently draped her leg over the top of the sofa to make a place for himself in the cradle of her thighs. He groaned as he sank into her moist depths, as he felt a pleasure so intense he was engulfed by it.

Rae cried out at the twin sensations of fire and ice rampaging through her. She knew only Jed could create this, and only he could quench it. Unconsciously, she clawed at his back, and he began to move inside her. She met each thrust with a fervent one of her own. She was aware of nothing but his hungry mouth on hers, his chest hard against her breasts, their hips stroking deeper and deeper in an ageless rhythm. Her body burned, and her flesh shivered, as raging red and icy blue sensations spiraled outward, mindlessly tossing her in their maelstrom. Jed's strong fingers gripped her thighs, and he chanted her name as he thrust into her one last time. Under her hands, his body shuddered almost violently. The fire and ice suddenly rushed together, breaking over her in wave after wave of ecstasy. It flooded her mind, coursed through her heart, and found the eddies of her soul. Then it pulled her under, tenderly enfolding her in its loving currents.

Rae became aware of her surroundings at the

same moment she became aware of a chuckle rumbling in Jed's chest.

"What's so funny?" she asked, feeling as if her body were floating.

"I was just thinking," he said, "that it was a good thing I knew you before only as a little girl. If you had been a few years older, you would have wreaked havoc with my adolescence. Lord, you're a dangerous woman."

She smiled into the warm skin of his shoulder. They lay together for a long moment in contented silence. Finally, she asked, "Jed?"

Her voice sounded unsure, and he knew that he had to dispel the doubts that were beginning to resurface. He raised his head and gazed down at her. She was so beautiful, he thought, and so vulnerable. Smiling, he smoothed her hair back and said, "I would never hurt you, sweetheart. Never. I promise."

She buried her face in his shoulder and nodded.

He would keep that promise, he vowed, as he held her in a tight embrace. She may not realize how much trust she had placed in him tonight, but he was well aware of it. He sensed that she had never allowed another man inside her barriers as she had him. To hurt her would be to hurt himself. It was awfully soon to make love, but they had both surrendered to a need that had been too strong to fight. He admitted that it was the best damn thing that had ever happened to him. He had no regrets.

Cool air wafted across his back, and he realized that the room was rapidly growing colder—or rather he was just beginning to notice it now.

"It's late, Rae, and you should be in a nice warm bed." He grimaced in disgust, knowing he wouldn't be joining her. The boys' presence had brought them together. Now, it would keep them apart.

Her arms tightened around his neck. "Not yet."

Jed decided he'd be a fool to protest. Concerned that his weight might be too much for her, he shifted to his side, keeping her between himself and the back of the sofa. Lazily stroking the slope of her hip, he said, "Now don't fall asleep, or else your nephews will get quite an anatomy lesson in the morning."

"Then you'd better stop what you're doing, because it feels too good," she said, tracing his collarbone with a forefinger.

He closed his eyes at the tingling sensation. "And you'd better stop what you're doing, otherwise I might do this."

He let his hand drift lower, his fingers spreading across her luscious derriere.

She leaned back and gazed up at him with knowing green-gray eyes. "Don't make any promises you can't keep, Jed."

He sensed that her teasing was an attempt to lighten her mood, and he was all for it. Pretense sometimes became reality—with a little help. He lightly kissed her nose. "Don't tempt me to try it. You'd be asleep halfway through the proceedings."

She opened her mouth to protest, but a yawn emerged instead. Covering her mouth with one hand, she sheepishly lowered her eyes.

"The prophet has spoken, my dear," he said, chuckling. "Time for bed. Besides, my tush is freezing."

She giggled again, and he rolled over to pick up the robes from the floor. Her white bikini underwear wasn't in the pile. Frowning, Jed leaned further over the edge of the sofa to check underneath its skirt. He leaned too far. Losing his balance, he slid right off the sofa and landed with a thump on the carpet. Surprised, he sat there for a moment. A short time ago, the couch hadn't seemed nearly so small.

Rae stretched toward the edge of the cushions and rested her chin in her fist. "Is your tush warmer now?"

He wondered if she knew what a beautiful picture she made, with her dark hair falling forward to frame her face, and her body gleaming like ivory in the glow of the lamp. He grinned at the mirth filling her eyes. "It's getting hotter by the minute."

"Probably just a rug burn, Jed. Nothing to get excited about."

Her full curving lips were inches from his, and unable to resist, he kissed them . . . slowly . . . leisurely. When he finally lifted his head, she gave a satisfied sigh.

"Now that's a rug burn, Jed."

"I know."

It was some time later that they reluctantly dressed and left the room. It was with even more reluctance that Rae watched him turn away from her bedroom door and continue down the hallway to the trophy room. He hesitated, his hand on the doorknob. In the darkened hallway, she sensed more than saw him give her one last look. Then he opened the door and slipped inside.

Once settled in her own bed, she found her body satiated and her mind restless with thoughts. She acknowledged she had created her own trap and had walked into it with her eyes wide open. Everything she'd done to keep her resistance up had had the opposite effect. She had been totally caught up in a sensual moment. . . .

Liar, she told herself in a sudden burst of honesty. She had allowed their lovemaking to happen— had wanted it to happen. In a lousy attempt at absolution, she had tried to convince herself she'd been "caught up" in something she never could have resisted. She had known what she was doing. From the beginning, her control had been almost nonexistent with Jed. Yet she'd gone right ahead and kidnapped him, allowed him to stay, and brought in her nephews who, instead of keeping them apart, had in a roundabout way actually thrown them together. If only there hadn't been a meeting of the Barkeley Club. If only Jed hadn't wanted to show her what he'd discovered in the reports. If only.

People had regretted those two particular words all their lives, she thought. She wasn't sure what she regretted—making love with Jed . . . or making love with her heart as well as her body.

Rae closed her eyes tightly against the thought.

Nine

"She's still sleepin'."

Michael's voice pulled Rae from a deep slumber. Not bothering to open her eyes, she mumbled, "Go watch cartoons."

She felt the edge of the mattress sink as the little boy climbed onto the bed. He crawled under the covers and snuggled against her back. She smiled to herself at the feel of his small pajama-clad body next to hers. Oh well, she thought, the cartoons were always worth a mention. Mark would probably be next. She hoped he wouldn't bounce on the bed as usual, but she knew the wish was in vain. She braced herself for the expected jolt.

"Here, you can get in on this side, Jed."

Her eyes flew open, and she sat bolt upright. Jed was standing at the foot of the bed with a huge grin on his face. Dressed in jeans and a blue sweater, he'd obviously been awake for quite some time. Momentarily speechless, she watched as his gaze drifted lower to the flimsy bodice of her satin nightgown. The amusement in his hazel eyes was instantly replaced by a hot glow. Memories of their lovemaking came back to her in a rush, and a heavy warmth flooded her body. She yanked the coverlet nearly to her chin, then turned to her nephew.

"Ah, Michael," she began, forcing herself to calm down and smile naturally. "I don't think Jed would like . . . I mean, Jed isn't interested . . . it's not a good idea, Michael."

"Why?" Michael asked.

The child's inevitable question, Rae thought. Now if only she could answer it without making an ass of herself.

"Because I was about to get up, anyway." She congratulated herself on her fast thinking. She usually functioned by rote before coffee.

"Oh."

Michael's disappointment was obvious. She sighed inwardly at the unhappy expression on his face. He had always liked to wake her up to snuggle and talk, and he evidently wanted to share that with Jed. Under the circumstances, though, it wasn't hard to be firm.

Reaching down, she brushed a stray lock of hair from Michael's forehead and said, "We could take a nap together this afternoon, okay?"

"Okay," Michael said, sitting up. "Just you, me, and Jed, though."

She suppressed a groan of frustration. Michael's friendship certainly knew no bounds. She glared at Jed, who hadn't spoken a word yet.

"I don't think Jed will be tired then," she said sweetly. "Will you, Jed?"

He stroked his mustache before answering. "It's hard to say— "

"Will you, Jed," she repeated forcefully.

"Well, the truth is—"

"Will you, Jed!"

"Maybe I'll—"

"Aaaaggh!"

Having vented her feelings, she flopped back on the pillow and pulled the covers over her head. It would be nice if lightning suddenly struck him, she thought. Or a bomb. She wasn't picky.

"Aunt Rae?"

She assumed it was Michael who was now rapping on her forehead through the quilt. "What?"

"Are you mad at me?"

"No, Michael."

"Are you mad at Jed?"

"No, Michael."

"I think we should give your aunt a little privacy," Jed said.

"Truer words were never spoken," Rae muttered into the bedclothes. As her nephew scrambled over her and off the bed, she poked her head out from under the covers.

"Michael," she whispered loudly. He turned around. "I need a good morning kiss."

Smiling, Michael scooted over to her and bussed her on the cheek. She snaked an arm out and yanked him on top of her, tickling him through the covers. Shrill giggles filled the room, as he squirmed and twisted away. Finally she stopped. Panting for breath, he settled down on her chest and leaned his forehead on hers. They stared at each other until she crossed her eyes. He giggled again.

Chuckling, she said, "Good morning, sweetie. Now beat it, so I can get up."

"Okay."

He shoved himself off her and ran over to Jed, who was staring at her with an odd expression on his face. For a wild second, she thought he was going to ask for a good morning kiss, too, but he just ushered her nephew out the door.

After they shut her bedroom door behind them, Rae groaned loudly and pulled the blanket back over her head. She wished she could stay there forever . . . or until Jed finally disappeared. Last night she hadn't considered how awkward it would be to see him again, but she'd never conceived of her own nephew inviting the man into her bed to snuggle and talk! She covered her face with her hands and shuddered. What a way to wake up. Jed's teasing hadn't helped any . . . or had it?

She lowered her hands. Any way would have been awkward—for her, at least. Jed handled embarrassing situations with aplomb. Luckily, Michael's innocent puzzlement and Jed's teasing had distracted her just enough to keep the awkwardness on a superficial level.

But what, she wondered frantically, would she say to him now? What did he think? More importantly, what was he feeling?

Shaking her head at the unanswerable questions, she acknowledged that matters were even more complicated between them now. They couldn't make love again. Jed was the wrong man at the wrong time and definitely in the wrong place. She'd have to make that very clear to him. What happened was just a result of physical attraction combined with close quarters. If and when . . .

No, she told herself. *If* and *when* meant she was looking ahead.

She had to deal with the present.

After lunch, Jed stood on the terrace in the shadows of the house and watched as Rae adroitly managed to avoid him for the third time in as many hours.

She was good, he thought, damn good at changing directions without actually seeming to. She had come through the French doors, spotted him at one end of the terrace, and waved before lightly running down the steps toward the maze. He doubted if anyone would have realized she hadn't been headed there in the first place, even though she'd had the straw basket on her arm. There was nothing in the maze to fill the basket with except hedge clippings.

Gazing down at the blooming chrysanthemums lining the terrace, he remembered how he'd decided to take a chance and talk to her that morning. He had actually had his hand on her bedroom doorknob when Michael came skipping down the hallway and proceeded to drag him into the room. Lord, she looked vulnerable—and sexy. The satin nightgown barely covered her coral-tipped breasts, and her eyes were wide with shock and surprise. He would have given anything to join her in her bed. Instead it was Michael who did. Little Michael! He still couldn't believe the hard shot of jealousy he felt watching her with her nephew. It was silly, of course, to be envious of a child. Michael was her nephew. But seeing her act so warm and affectionate with someone other than him had almost driven him to distraction. He was the one who should have been in that bed, dammit! They could have talked, sorted everything out.

He knew he had handled the rest of the morning all wrong. He shouldn't have waited, hoping she'd come to him, but he wanted to give her time to adjust to the fact that they'd made love. She turned it into a game of avoidance. At the moment, though, there was really nothing he could do. Not with the nephews around. Any discussion was bound to be interrupted. The French doors opened again, and he looked up to see Burrows coming through them.

"Good afternoon, sir."

Jed muttered a greeting before turning his head to stare at the maze. He knew it was better to wait until nothing could interrupt them. Tonight, he promised himself. They'd straighten quite a few things out then. Tonight, when the boys were gone.

"Have you found an alternate site yet for your construction project, sir?"

Jed turned back. Burrows was adjusting a white wrought-iron chair under the table.

"What?"

"I said, have you—"

"I got the question," Jed said, interrupting the butler. "How do you know what I've been doing?"

Burrows straightened, and fixed a stern glare on him. "I am not a dunce, sir."

"No, you're not," Jed agreed, realizing that the butler probably knew enough to guess the rest. "Burrows, can I ask you something?"

"Of course, sir."

"Did you ever find yourself trying to climb a wall while someone was kicking the blocks out from under you?"

"Once, sir." Burrows gave him a ghost of a smile. "It was in Greece during the war. Mr. Merriman and I were trapped on a cave ledge for twenty-two hours while a platoon of German soldiers took shelter inside the cave to avoid a snowstorm. We could hardly kill fifty men before they killed us. If I may use your analogy, sir, we didn't even have the slight advantage of a wall. You see, I had a bad cold at the time. One cough and we were dead men."

In amazement, Jed asked, "What the hell were you two doing in Greece during the war?"

"Spying, sir," the small man replied matter-of-factly. "Mr. Merriman and I were on a joint mission for the American and British governments. We were ever so grateful to see those soldiers finally pack up and leave." Burrows smiled another tiny smile. "They left us quite a nice path through the snow. We barely got our feet wet."

Jed almost laughed at the idea of Merriman and Burrows as James Bond-like spies. It was outrageous. Still, Burrows had never struck him as a man to tell tales.

"I take it, sir, that you are having difficulties with Miss Rachel."

Jed shoved his hands in his jacket pockets. "I wish it was just difficulties, Burrows. Patience is getting me nowhere fast."

Burrows shook his head. "You're overlooking the obvious, sir."

"There is no obvious," Jed snapped in frustration, as he leaned back against the wall of the house.

"Miss Rachel's behavior has been quite obvious, and so has yours. Consider that, sir."

Now what, Jed wondered, did Burrows mean by "obvious" behavior? What had they done? . . .

He realized exactly what they had done, and he glanced up sharply only to find Burrows had gone. Jed swore. Somehow, the butler had discovered that he and Rae had made special use of the drawing room last night. He doubted there was very much that Burrows didn't know—about anything. As the man said: he wasn't a dunce. Even the boys probably sensed there was something more going on between him and Rae than a simple kidnapping. Although Michael didn't understand the nuances of their relationship, the five-year-old was so attuned to them that he was acting almost like a matchmaker, and doing a damn good job of it. Face it, Jed told himself, he and Rae hadn't done much to hide their strong attraction to each other. That was obvious. The conflict between them over the estate had also produced some rather bizarre behavior too. That Rae had kidnapped him was bizarre enough, but he'd taken it a giant step further by insisting on remaining kidnapped. Setting foot on this property was like stepping into a loony bin. Both of them were certainly giving Merriman a run for his money in the eccentricity department.

Setting foot on the property . . .

Stepping into a loony bin . . .

It was the house! The house made people do crazy things. He had heard of houses being possessed by poltergeists, but this one must be possessed by an eccentricity bug that made people behave like loonies. Merriman had bought the house as a young man, and he probably hadn't been eccentric then, but now the man was noted for it. Rae hadn't even been in the house a month before she was kidnapping people. Of course, she had had years of exposure to the place. He was working against his own company for her, and Burrows, who should be on her side, seemed to be on his. Impossible and insane. It was definitely the house. That was the only explanation. Nothing else made sense.

He heard light footsteps coming up the steps of the terrace, and knowing it must be Rae, he decided one piece of insanity had gone on long enough. As she reached the top step, she nodded to him and headed for the French doors.

"Rae."

She stopped for an instant at his call, then continued on her way, saying, "I'm sorry, Jed, but I have to make an important phone call."

Jed strode over and took her arm before she could disappear inside. "Wait. This is more important than a phone call. You have to listen to me—"

"There's nothing to discuss—"

"I think Burrows knows we made love last night."

Her eyes widened in shock, and she sputtered, "But that's impossible! Everyone was asleep." She gripped his arm. "Do you think he saw . . . ?"

He curved his arm around her shoulders in comfort. "No. He just said our behavior was obvious. We haven't exactly been hiding our attraction to each other. Face it, Rae, anyone could have figured it out. But his saying that made me think about the way we've been behaving over the estate too. Have you ever kidnapped anyone before? Even thought of it? Or done anything even remotely as crazy? Not something a little wild or silly, but something really off the wall."

She shook her head.

"See. Your behavior is obvious. I've never done anything off the wall, either, but now I'm risking my job to find another site and insisting on staying kidnapped. Then there's your uncle. Merriman's been mad as a hatter for a long time. What about when he was younger, before he bought this place?"

"I don't know. He used to say he never had any fun." She frowned at him. "Why?"

"I think it's the house, Rae. It makes people do crazy things. There's something wrong with—"

The look on her face stopped his words. Her beautiful features were set with a blank expression. The only giveaway was her chin. It quivered as she tried to suppress her amusement. Suddenly she burst into hysterical laughter. She buried her face in his shoulder, her body shaking with mirth. He glared down at the top of her head.

"Dammit, Rae! Will you get serious?"

"I . . . can't!" she gasped in between fits of laughter.

He turned her to face him, and grasping both shoulders, gently shook her. "I know it sounds crazy, but think about it. Think about what Burrows said. And Michael . . . even he—"

Her amusement immediately stopped, and with a horrified moan, she pushed out of his arms. "Oh, no! Michael saw us too?"

"No, of course not! I just meant that even he's aware of something strange going on, and he responds to it."

She slumped in relief. "Thank goodness! Michael is too young to understand the birds and the bees, let alone visual aids. I have been meaning to talk to you, though, about . . . about what happened."

"Then why have you been avoiding me?" he asked in disbelief, forgetting all thoughts about the house being possessed.

"I haven't."

"Sure, you haven't."

She waved a hand in dismissal. "I admit I'm attracted to you, Jed. That fact surprised me, and I guess I was . . ." She made a face. "Let's just say, it was a combination of things. The point is, we're not going to make love again."

Jed stared at her. "We're not?"

"No," she said flatly. "We're not."

There was a long silence. Finally, he said, "That's it? Just we're not?"

"That's right. Just we're not."

Jed said nothing, because he was afraid of what he *would* say. He knew he shouldn't be surprised by her reaction. As Burrows would say: her behavior had been obvious. She was still being obvious. Even after last night, she was still refusing to acknowledge there was something special between them. From her tense stance, he realized she was more than ready to fight him on the subject. He considered all his options and the risks involved with each, then decided on the one she'd least expect.

"Okay."

Her jaw dropped open in clear astonishment. "You . . . you agree?"

"Absolutely. You don't have to explain anything, Rae. Not a thing. I understand completely, and I just want to say thank you for being mature and sensible." He patted her shoulder, then opened the French doors. "You'd better go make that phone call now."

"What phone . . . oh, yes, the phone call." She turned toward the open doors. She turned back and gazed at him in bewilderment. Jed kept his smile friendly. She turned around and walked into the house, while muttering something incomprehensible under her breath.

Jed shut the doors after her. He grinned. It wouldn't be long before she'd be furious with him for *not* fighting her on the subject. If she reacted the way he hoped, they'd be doing more than talking tonight.

•   •   •

Hours later, Jed paced the darkness of the trophy room. So much for reverse psychology, he thought in disgust as he brushed against a stuffed moosehead.

Rae hadn't reacted the way he'd expected. She hadn't reacted at all. At first, he'd been pleased at the way she shot him dirty looks all afternoon. He knew she was building to a confrontation, and he knew she was only waiting for the opportunity to let loose. But when the boys left for home shortly after dinner, she immediately excused herself, claiming a sick headache. Something had gone wrong, and he had no idea what. He'd be damned, though, before they went back to the beginning. He wanted her. He needed her. And the more he wanted her, the more he needed her. Her excusing herself was a clear rejection, just as her attitude had been all day. Either that, or she thought he was crazy for telling her the house was possessed.

Hell, he thought, this had nothing to do with the house. Stick to the obvious. They had something unique together. It transcended their differences over the estate. It was something that couldn't be denied. Yet, she was denying them both. She had no right to do that, and it was about damn time she learned it.

He strode over to the trophy room door.

She couldn't sleep. She knew it was useless to try, but she reshaped her pillow anyway, and rolled onto her side. She closed her eyes and attempted to clear her mind of everything but rolling green pastures.

Their behavior was obvious.

With a loud groan, Rae rolled onto her back. Those words just wouldn't go away.

She acknowledged that her behavior had certainly been obvious today. She'd acted like a teenage girl embarrassed to face a boy after a first date. In spite of her resolve of the morning, she just hadn't known how to broach the subject without making a fool of herself. Well, she'd done that by avoiding him in the first place. When she finally confronted him on the terrace, she wound up looking even more foolish. And being told she was mature and sensible had only bewildered and aggravated her. She'd spent the rest of the time wanting to smack his face—or something equally as satisfying. She probably would have, too, if Burrows's words hadn't kept coming back to her. After her brother had picked up the boys, she couldn't stand it any longer. A headache hadn't been far from the truth, she admitted. The need to be alone and think had been pounding through her by then. Unfortunately, her thoughts had circled in her brain like a merry-go-round.

Obvious behavior.

She remembered Jed's notion that the house caused people to act crazily, and a giggle escaped her. Lord, he could make her laugh, and if he wasn't making her laugh, he was making her want him so badly that she thought she *would* go crazy. The moment she had uttered the words "We won't," she knew she wanted to say exactly the opposite.

She'd been attracted to men before, but she'd always been in control. Not with Jed, though. Something more than physical chemistry drew her to him. She'd tried to ignore it at first, then tried to guard herself from it, and finally, she'd tried to fight it. Last night, she'd surrendered to it, and, dammit, she still didn't know what it was. She only knew that with each minute that passed she was drawn in deeper.

Yet it was supposed to be obvious.

"Oh, my God!" Rae gasped, and shot upright as realization dawned.

Moaning, she covered her face with shaking hands and tried to calm herself. She couldn't possibly be in love with Jed. It was all wrong, there were so many problems . . . and yet it was so obvious. In spite of everything, she'd fallen in love with him. She could feel the rightness of it in her bones. How, she wondered wildly, had it happened? When? She didn't bother with why, since she had no answers to the first two questions.

Leaning back against the pillows, she lowered her hands from her face and acknowledged that there was no sense denying that she loved him. She'd even known it the previous night when she worried that her heart was involved. She hadn't been able to face it then. She had to face it now.

The door to her bedroom suddenly opened, and she recognized Jed's silhouette on the threshold. Without a word, he shut the door behind him and strode over to the side of her bed. He yanked his sweater over his head and dropped it on the door. His hands went to his waist. She heard the snap of his jeans being pulled open. Any thoughts of protesting died at his actions. She stared, wide-eyed, at the virile shadow he made as he quickly shed the rest of his clothes. Naked, he lifted the covers and slid into the bed. She sensed his determination and need, and knew she couldn't deny him. She loved him.

She had never felt so vulnerable before in her life.

Then his arms were around her, and she knew she'd never felt so safe.

Ten

Much later, Rae lay exhausted in Jed's arms. Breathing in the musky scent of their lovemaking, she smiled to herself as she lazily stroked the muscles of his back. He had taken her with him to an even sweeter oblivion this time, and she didn't regret one moment of it. However, there was one tiny detail which had to be cleared up.

"I thought," she finally murmured in amusement, "that you agreed we weren't going to do this again."

His lips had been caressing the soft column of her neck, and she felt him grin against her skin.

"I lied."

She laughed softly. "You cad, Jed Waters. To think, I trusted you to behave yourself."

He kissed her for a long moment, then said, "Do you trust me, Rae?"

For a second, her insides tensed at his question. She trusted him with her life. If she were in danger, the only person she'd want at her side would be Jed, and she did trust him to protect her as best he could from his company's interests in the estate. It was her heart that made her hesitate answering him. Could she trust him with her heart?

Reaching up, she touched his mustache and said, "Yes, I trust you. I trust you to do your best not to hurt me—in any way."

His mouth tenderly covered hers, and she sensed not only his gratitude at her admission, but his promise not to betray her fragile offering.

Finally, he lifted his head. "Work with me to find a new site, Rae. I think we've been working against each other long enough." He rubbed a hair-roughened leg against the sensitive flesh on the inside of her thigh as he added, "Wanna bet the farm that we'd be hell together outside the bedroom too?"

Laughing, she said, "You don't have a farm, Jed."

"A little hedging never hurt anyone," he drawled, nuzzling her neck. His hand drifted to her breast. "Ready for some more obvious behavior?"

"Always."

As he pulled her closer, she wondered if Jed's "behavior" was as obvious as hers. It had to be, she firmly told herself.

It had to be.

The sounds of someone moving about the bedroom sifted through the layers of Jed's sleep, and he opened one eye. He instantly closed it against the bright morning sunlight streaming through the bedroom windows. Before he closed his eye, though, he glimpsed Burrows setting a coffee tray on the nightstand.

Dammit, he thought blearily, why the hell . . .

His morning fog immediately cleared. He swore under his breath, knowing Rae would be embarrassed that the butler had discovered them. He'd intended to be a gentleman and sneak back into the trophy room, but with each moment it had been harder to let go of the night.

Very carefully, so he wouldn't disturb Rae, who was still sleeping, he raised his head and put a finger to his lips to hush Burrows, then motioned toward the bedroom door.

Without a word or even a nod of acknowledgement, Burrows set a newspaper next to the tray and left the room.

Puzzled, Jed frowned for a moment, then shrugged. Just as long as the man was gone, he thought. He turned back to the woman sleeping next to him. One bare shoulder was exposed from under the satin coverlet, tempting him to kiss it. He did, then tenderly lifted the strands of dark hair away from her face. Her features gleamed like fragile ivory in the morning light. He couldn't imagine a time when he would not be in awe of her beauty. Rachel Barkeley had become an obsession, and he never wanted to be free of her.

"Rae," he whispered giving her a gentle shake, as the aroma of hot coffee filled the room. "Coffee."

She mumbled something unintelligible and rolled over on her stomach. Jed admired the soft line of her spine and decided the heck with the coffee.

He leaned over, and starting at the nape of her neck, kissed his way down the lovely length of feminine back. He pushed the covers lower. Rae finally stirred. Sighing, she rolled over, and he found himself faced with the delightful decision of which breast to honor first.

"Good morning," she murmured in a low sexy voice, opening her eyes. Her hands began to trace patterns on his shoulders.

He gave her a wicked smile. "Good morning."

The sight of her, sleepy and contented, was too much for him, and he bent his head. . . .

"Do I smell coffee?" she asked, just as his lips were about to enclose one pouting nipple.

Jed smothered a groan at her reminder of Burrows's visit. He raised his head. "About the coffee . . . Burrows brought it."

Her eyes widened, and she glanced over at the nightstand and saw the coffee service. Returning her gaze to him, she asked hesitantly, "Burrows was here?"

He nodded. "I'm sorry, Rae. I meant to go back to the trophy room—"

"I'm glad you didn't." She touched his mustache. "Very glad." She chuckled and added, "Anyway, I doubt if Burrows was surprised."

Jed grinned at her, privately pleased that she was accepting their relationship. "Well, his eyebrows didn't shoot off the top of his head."

She sat up against the headboard, pulling the satin coverlet with her. Reaching over to the nightstand, she lifted the already filled cup from the tray and took a sip. Leaning back, she closed her eyes and sighed. "Bless the man. Good hot coffee."

Jed made a face. "What about me?"

Opening her eyes again, she held out the cup to him. "There's only one cup. I suppose we'll have to share."

"I didn't mean—"

The bedroom door swung open again. He immediately checked that he and Rae were properly covered, then watched in disgust as Burrows entered the room carrying another cup and saucer. A newspaper was tucked under his arm, and the dogs followed behind him. Samson immediately headed for Jed's side of the bed, while Delilah sat at the foot. Jed wondered if Rae's bedroom was doubling as a train station. Everybody seemed to wander into it at the damnedest times.

"Good morning, miss," Burrows said. "It is a beautiful day, although chilly."

Seemingly not bothered by his presence, Rae greeted him in return.

The butler set the cup and newspaper next to the tray. "Will there be anything else, miss?"

"Nothing, thank you."

The butler turned and left the room.

"Doesn't he know how to knock?" Jed asked, as he petted Samson's massive head.

"True butlers never knock, Jed," she said, with a gleam of laughter in her eyes. "They simply shut the door again if they're about to interrupt something they shouldn't. Also, they never see or hear anything which would cause embarrassment; their only job is to anticipate their employers' comfort. My father used to say good butlers were like priests. They never betrayed your secrets."

"I'll keep it in mind next time I have to make a

confession," he said, smiling wryly, then pointed to the nightstand. "Now that I seem to have my own cup, how about pouring?"

"Bossy. You'll probably want this, too." She handed him one of the newspapers, and after pouring the coffee, passed the cup.

The coffee was strong and still hot, nearly burning his tongue when he sipped the brew. Glancing at the headlines, he said, "This has got to be the second best way to wake up." He turned and leered at her. "You are the first."

She chuckled. "Flatterer."

Giving the dogs a glance, he said, "And much as I would like to wake up both ways this morning, I have no desire to give an X-rated performance in front of the dogs. Or Burrows."

"I should hope not. Can I borrow this?" Without waiting for his answer, she picked up the business section of the paper and flipped through the pages, stopping at the stock market quotes.

"Watching your stocks?" he asked dryly. There were definite drawbacks to luxury, he acknowledged.

"My clients', actually. Damn! KSL is down another quarter."

Surprised, Jed set his cup back on the saucer. "Since when are you a stockbroker?"

She grinned at him. "Since I was twenty-one. You know that."

"Rae," he said patiently. "I knew a lot about you as a child, and I know that you are an intelligent, sexy, gentle, loving, honorable, stubborn—"

"Stubborn!" she exclaimed.

"Woman," he continued unperturbed. "But you've neglected a few dry facts, sweetheart."

"Good thing you said 'intelligent' first," she grumbled, shoving the paper aside. "I'm also a licensed stockbroker."

"You're kidding!"

She frowned at him. "What's the matter? Don't I look intelligent enough for that?"

"Of course you do," he said hastily. "I guess I have this stereotyped view that wealthy people don't work at anything."

"They do, if they had a father like mine." There was a faraway smile on her face. "He believed in giving his children what he called 'seed money.' It was actually an investment in our ability, since we had to start our own businesses with it and pay him a cut of the profits. Figuring the overhead would be low and profits high, I got some friends to let me invest *their* money on the stock market." She chuckled. "You should have seen my father's face when he found out what my older brother did with his."

"What?" Jed asked, curious.

"Ever hear of the Living Fit Woman exercise spas?"

He nodded.

"Well, that's Rand; he owns the chain. I think we bewildered my father with our choices." She was silent for a moment. "He died last year."

"I know," Jed said. "I read it in the papers at the time. I'm sorry, Rae."

She smiled. "You would have liked him, Jed. Anyway, that's about it for dry facts, unless you want to see my college diploma. Oh! I own a small townhouse in Manhattan that I'll probably be selling now. What are your dry facts?"

Jed laughed. "I'm a fairly well-adjusted man, who has very few vices since I gave up smoking three years ago. I have an apartment in Center City, no debts, and money in the bank. I guess you could say I'm well off, although not wealthy."

"Does it bother you that I am?" she asked as a worried frown crossed her brow.

"No. I figure you didn't ask for it, so it's not your fault."

"Chauvinist."

He dipped his head. "Thank you. I also like to lie naked in bed with an equally naked you and discuss dry facts."

He leaned over and kissed her leisurely. Her arms crept around his neck, as their lips clung to each other with morning passion. . . .

Samson woofed, breaking them apart.

"I think he's telling us we should get up," Rae said in dry amusement. "I guess we should. I have to 'stockmarket' first before I help you with our problem."

Wrapping the coverlet around her, she slid out of bed and headed for the bathroom.

Jed gave the dog a dirty look.

"Phoebe, you need to have your money hidden away right now," Rae repeated for the fourth time to her sobbing client. Seated behind the antique Hepplewhite desk in the library, she eyed the stock price updates scrolling up her computer screen and wished that it was still Sunday. No wonder it

was called Blue Monday, she thought in exasperation, knowing Jed was in the drawing room working just as hard on the site problem.

"Eric's lawyer is insisting on a three-million-
dollar settlement!" Phoebe Collins wailed into the
phone, shattering Rae's thoughts. "He says that
would have been Eric's potential earnings if he
hadn't married me. Eric's last play was *The Season of the Bear*, and it flopped off Broadway. He
hasn't written a thing since, but I didn't care
about that, Rae. I loved him so much. He's claiming I smother his creative flow!"

Rae readjusted the receiver against her sore ear.
Phoebe's husbands got greedier with every divorce,
she thought, and glanced heavenwards for divine
guidance. "I know that the last thing you want to
think about right now is your stocks, but you're
going to have to, Phoebe."

"No! I—"

Rae broke in. "They can help you now. People
not only make investments to make more money,
they also make investments because they don't
want other people to get all their money. With
Eric asking for such a large settlement, the last
thing you need to do is to show earnings."

"So how do I avoid that?" the woman asked
with a sniffle.

At last, Rae thought, Phoebe was listening. She
proceeded to explain potential growth investments.
The trick, though, was in the growing. "Check
with your lawyer, but I think you'll find that he'll
agree about offering Eric a reasonable cash settlement and a block or blocks of shares in a firm
that has the potential to reach the sum Eric is

asking for. A new fashion house, or a wildcat oil company, maybe. Something along those lines. Of course, it would have to be with people who had already proven their know-how in the business, otherwise Eric and his lawyer wouldn't touch it."

"But Eric could make millions and millions if the wells come in!"

"There is that," Rae conceded. "It all depends on whether he's willing to take a risk, Phoebe. In either event, your outlay would be much less at settlement, and you can probably write it off as a loss over several years." Keeping her voice neutral, she added, "Of course, should the stock pay off and Eric make millions and millions, his financial situation will be entirely different. I would imagine that you could sue for alimony at that point."

Phoebe gasped loudly. "Find something good, and I'll drain the bum for every cent he makes!"

When Rae finally hung up the phone, she couldn't help chuckling. Phoebe was out for revenge now. Still, it was the woman's own fault for falling in love with the wrong man.

Her amusement faded, when she remembered that only yesterday she'd thought Jed was the wrong man. Jed was the right man at the wrong time. Not the wrong time, she amended, knowing that there was never a wrong time for love. They just had a little problem with the estate. All they had to do was find the solution.

She reminded herself she had another little problem with Jed. She didn't know if he felt the same way she did. She forced the thought out of her head. It was better to take one problem at a time. Once the estate was out of the way, then she could concentrate on Jed.

Burrows came into the room and set a coffee tray on her desk. Rae grinned at it, doubting if she'd ever be able to think of coffee without thinking of Burrows.

"The cleaning service has arrived, miss." He tightened his lips. "I hope that they will do a proper job this time."

"Let me know if they don't, and I'll speak to whoever is in charge," she said. She privately admitted that the cleaning service could hose the place down with industrial-strength disinfectant, and Burrows would still grumble.

The butler nodded, then cleared his throat. "Mr. Jed moved several of his things into your bedroom, miss."

She knew Burrows was obliquely asking about the change in household arrangements. She also knew that he was signifying his approval of Jed by using his first name, and she hid a smile of pleasure. "That's fine, Burrows."

The phone rang, and she groaned. It was probably Phoebe again, wanting her to buy shares in some wild venture that might pay billions. Waving Burrows away from it, she picked up the receiver.

"Barkeley residence. Rachel Barkeley speaking." Knowing Burrows was a stickler for proper telephone etiquette, she grinned at his look of approval as he left the room.

"Well now, this must be my lucky day," boomed a jovial male voice into her ear. "I was calling for Jed, but frankly, young lady, I've been wanting to speak to you for some time now. I'm Henry Morrison, president of Atlantic Developers."

Rae stiffened. She forced herself to relax.

"You are speaking to me now, Mr. Morrison," she said coolly. "What can I do for you?"

"It's about this mess your uncle made with his running off to that monastery. I'm sure you're as unhappy about it as I am. Now, I'm a believer in the theory that any dispute can be resolved quickly . . . unless, of course, the lawyers get to it first." This time hearty laughter boomed across the wire. "Wouldn't do to let them draw it out for years, while confusing the issue all out of proportion."

She gritted her teeth to hold back the angry words at his subtle threat. "I do see your point, Mr. Morrison."

"I thought you might. The moment I heard your voice, I knew you would be a sensible young woman. Businesslike too. I appreciate that in a person. I think that we can just solve the whole shebang if I give you a figure and you tell me if it's in line with what you would be willing to sell the estate for." He named a sum.

"That's very generous, Mr. Morrison," she said slowly, drawing on her years of training in business to remain calm. It was a good thing he was on the other end of a phone line, she thought, otherwise he would be on the other end of a punch in the nose. She added, "However, I'm afraid you've left me a little confused."

"Confused?"

"Yes, sir. I am wondering why your vice president is diligently searching for a site to replace the estate, while you are offering a price for it. You *are* from Atlantic Developers, aren't you?"

"Yes, I'm from Atlantic!" he snapped.

"Well, I suspect some communication lines have crossed at the company, and you probably haven't gotten the message—"

"Now just one—"

"Excuse me, sir," she broke in politely. "All I was going to say was that I have no intention of selling the estate. I'm sorry for your time and trouble—"

"Now you listen to me, missy. I made an agreement of sale for that place, and I don't give a damn whose signature is on the settlement papers, but they will be signed! You think about that!"

"Shall I tell Mr. Waters to stop looking for another site?" she asked sweetly.

"Jed already knows what I want!" Morrison nearly shouted. "And what I send him after, he gets! No matter what it takes! You think about that too!"

The words stabbed deeply into her, and she nearly cried out at the sudden pain. She wanted desperately to deny them, but her voice was frozen. Everything inside her had frozen at the thought that Jed would do *anything* to get the estate from her. It just couldn't be true. She loved him. She trusted him. . . .

She was aware of Morrison speaking again.

"We're getting away from the point here, Miss Barkeley. It just seems to me that we can come to some kind of arrangement without the lawyers using their muckraking tactics, but I do understand your hesitation." She realized his voice was much calmer, almost soothing. "After all, selling a house isn't like tossing an old dress in the trash, is it? You just take your time considering my offer and give me a call back. Now I suppose I better talk to Jed and find out what he's up to."

Rae finally found her voice. "Yes. Yes, of course."

She put the receiver down very gently on the desktop and went in search of the man who had well and truly caught her in his trap.

Eleven

"It's hopeless, Jed," Rae said later that afternoon, as she dropped some site reports onto the living room coffee table.

Seated across from her, he chuckled. "Just impossible, sweetheart, but never hopeless."

Her heart lifted at the endearment, and she immediately suppressed the feeling. Picking up another set of papers, she gazed at them, but her thoughts were on the morning's revelations.

It wasn't the first time she'd gone over it in her mind, and she knew it wouldn't be the last. After she'd told Jed his boss was on the telephone, she hid herself away in the library again. When the emotional shock was finally under control, she considered what she should do. She quickly realized the one thing she shouldn't do was divulge what Morrison had blurted out. As much pleasure as it would have given her to tell Jed what a rat he was and toss him off the premises, it would be an even greater pleasure to beat him at his own game. So she said nothing. Jed could *think* he was making a fool of her, but she had too much pride to reveal he'd nearly been successful.

With an inner smile, she acknowledged Morrison had blundered very badly with his offer. In another week's time, Jed would have probably romanced the place out from under her. He must have been furious with his boss, but he'd never brought the subject up. At first, she was surprised, then she realized it was a very shrewd move on his part. He'd already mentioned Atlantic's continued interest in the estate several times and could have excused the offer as Morrison's overactive enthusiasm. Or he could have continued making himself out as the hero protecting her from the bad guys. In fact, there were any number of ways he could have smoothed it over. By not saying anything, however, Jed did seem to be the one in charge, not Morrison.

She blessed her mother for the years of training on how to maintain a cool, poised facade in the face of disaster. Since she'd joined him in the living room, she'd been giving quite a performance. She was positive he hadn't noticed a thing wrong, but the hurt and anger inside her had built with every tender look and caress he'd given her.

Let it build, she thought. Eventually, it would wall off her heart.

"How about going out for dinner and a movie?" he asked, breaking into her thoughts.

She glanced up to find him grinning at her. "Tonight?"

"I suppose we *could* do it tomorrow morning."

There was a devilish glint in his hazel eyes. "It all depends on how much you want to take Merriman's place as Resident Eccentric."

She couldn't help the smile that curved her lips. "No, thank you, I believe Burrows is already preparing dinner."

"Okay, then the movie." He reached across the small table and took her hand. She controlled herself not to yank it from his warm, strong grasp. "We've been interrupted enough by dogs and boys and butler and work, Rae. We need a little time to ourselves."

It was on the tip of her tongue to say she was too tired, when she realized it might sound suggestive. So far, she'd managed not to think about how she'd keep him out of her bed, without really looking the fool. Maybe a movie wasn't such a bad idea, after all. She'd have two hours in a darkened theater to come up with an acceptable excuse— and she wouldn't have to guard her facial expressions while doing so.

"I think you're right. A movie sounds wonderful."

She hoped *Bambi* was playing somewhere. The last thing she wanted to see was some damn love story.

"*A Man And A Woman!*"

"Yep," Jed said, as he steered the car past the movie marquee and into the theater parking lot. "It's a terrific movie."

"I know that," she said in an exasperated voice. "But obviously you've seen it before, and so have I. There's that new horror movie at—"

"Rachel Barkeley, I'm surprised at you!" he teased, while maneuvering the car into a parking spot. He turned off the ignition. "This is one of the greatest movies of all time, a true classic, and you want to pass it up for blood and guts. For shame!"

"Well, it's just that we've both seen it before," she mumbled, not looking at him.

"But not together."

He got out of the car and walked around to the passenger side to open the door for her. She didn't say anything as she got out and waited for him to close the door.

"Come on," he coaxed, taking her arm. "I'll even treat you to some candy."

She sighed and began walking with him to the box office. "Anybody ever tell you you're the last of the red hot dates, Jed?"

"Of course," he replied. "In the eighth grade, I took Marylou Polaski to the Autumn Dance, and she thought I was the best slow dancer there."

"Oh yeah?" she asked, grinning triumphantly up at him. "Any other 'hot' dates, besides good old Marylou?"

"I'm not a dope. Beyond eighth grade, I plead the fifth."

Just after they settled themselves in the back of the nearly empty theater, the movie began. Jed handed Rae the box of candy to hold and draped his arm across the back of her seat.

"Candy?" Rae asked, offering up the box.

"Thanks."

With his free hand, he dug inside for several pieces of the gummy candy and popped them into his mouth. As he watched the bittersweet love affair unfold on the screen, he decided he had been right about their needing some time away from the house. He sensed that something was bothering her, as she helped him sort through the various property projections. When she called it hopeless, he knew she was dejected that there was no quick solution in sight. Over the years, he'd learned to have patience with seemingly impossible problems. Still, he could easily understand her frustration with this one. The one time he really needed a quick fix, none was forthcoming, dammit! In spite of how close they'd become, the deal was still between them, and it would continue to be.

Then there was Henry nearly crowing with delight that his vice president was ensconced at the Barkeley estate. He'd been half-expecting Henry to get in touch with him, even though he'd told his assistant, Ross, to say he was in Harrisburg. Ross would never hold out against Henry, and who could blame him? Henry had had a good laugh over the kidnapping, but it had taken quite a bit to convince him that the new objective of finding an alternate site remained unchanged.

At least, his boss had said he hadn't spoken with Rae, Jed thought in relief. He could just imagine the conversation if he had, but he knew Rae would have told him if anything had been said. Knowing Rae, she would have set the dogs on him again. Their relationship was fragile and complicated enough, without Henry trampling over it.

Clearing his mind of pressures, he relaxed and congratulated himself once again on thinking of a movie. *A Man And A Woman* had been the perfect choice, he thought as he hummed along with the famous mandolin theme.

Between them, they finished off the candy about halfway through the movie. Rae crumbled the box, then leaned over and whispered, "Ever notice how the food never lasts through the movie?"

"They do it that way on purpose to leave time for 'making out,' " Jed said, while he ran his fingers through the strands of her heavy, lustrous hair. "I forgot to tell you, but this is a great movie for necking too."

"Jed!"

Ignoring her protest, he pulled her closer and kissed her. His mustache brushed enticingly against her mouth. For a moment, she struggled against the desire coursing through her, then relaxed. He deepened the kiss, letting his tongue swirl with hers to the rhythm of the theme music. Her arms crept around his neck, and her lips clung to his for long moments. Finally, he shifted to string kisses along her jaw.

"We're much too old for this," she murmured, her arms tightening as he kissed the sweet shell of her ear.

"Nothing like a little necking in a movie to revitalize the aged," he whispered.

As his mouth covered hers again, Rae knew she had made a terrible miscalculation. She had thought her anger and hurt would keep her detached. In a way, she was. Half of her watched in shock as the other half melted from the sweet fire he was creating. Feeling the slow wave of heat flooding her veins, she wondered how she could love a man and hate him at the same time. It was a contradiction, she thought dimly. But she was helpless to resist him. She'd walked into this trap with her eyes wide open, and now her love for him was closing off any escape route. At twenty-seven, she had had enough experience not to love until she could trust, but she'd followed her heart first with Jed. She was still following it.

Even as she stroked his shoulders, she knew that what she had now with Jed would never be enough, and what she wanted with him she would never have.

In the small hours of the night, as he held her in his sleeping embrace, she realized that she was old enough to know that love didn't come in a perfect package.

She would take what she could before it was gone.

Jed woke with a sudden start. Instantly alert, he lay for a moment, listening for whatever had disturbed him. Rae slept unmoving in the crook of his arm, and he finally opened his eyes.

The curtains were still closed, although he could see the gray-pink light of early morning filtering through them. There was no coffee tray on the nightstand, so he knew it hadn't been Burrows who had disrupted his sleep. Attempting to go back to sleep was useless. He thought of kissing Rae awake, then decided it would be gentlemanly to let her sleep.

He slipped out of bed and dressed quietly, before leaving the room. The dogs, hearing his footsteps in the upper hall, met him halfway up the back stairs that led to the kitchen. Samson greeted him with his tail wagging, but Delilah was still snubbing him. Downstairs, he took his sweatshirt jacket from the pantry room peg and went out the kitchen door. The dogs rushed past him through the open doorway.

The autumn morning was chilly, almost too chilly for just the jacket. Jed walked briskly down the back lawn to the river in an attempt to warm himself. He stopped to admire the turning foliage in the park on the opposite bank. In another month the leaves would all be gone. Still, the view was stunning with the morning mists rising from the river, and the surrounding stillness gave him a sense of peace and contentment.

The dogs suddenly stopped sniffing around a tree and scrambled off in the direction of the house. Jed turned around to see Burrows making his way down the back lawn to the herb garden. He'd noticed the other day that one section of it was nothing but a lump of mud, but with everything else happening it had seemed a trivial thing.

He walked across the lawn and joined the butler on one of the garden walkways.

"I didn't think anyone else was up but me," he said. "Beautiful day, isn't it?"

"Yes, sir, it is," Burrows said, although there was a slight tightening around his mouth. "I had hoped that this damaged section of the garden would have begun to dry out."

Jed glanced over at the muddy area which was about six feet wide. He remembered when he'd seen Rae on the day he snuck in looking for

Merriman. Smiling at the memory of her mud-streaked face and slender form, he said, "I remember Rae saying something about a damaged water line. I take it this is where it happened."

Burrows nodded. "I do know a little about gardening, but not enough to cope with this. Unlike most of my fellow countrymen, I have no green thumb. If you'll beg my pardon for saying so, at the moment I cannot help wishing Miss Rachel had kidnapped your father instead of you, sir. He would know how to salvage the bed."

Jed chuckled. "Somehow, I don't see my mother sitting still while Pop is kidnapped by a beautiful young woman."

He smothered a laugh, as the other man said, "More's the pity. Your father took great pride in the care he gave to these grounds."

"Well, I was forced to specialize in holly trees around here," Jed said, bending down on one knee and pressing his hand into the wet soil. "But I can tell you this ground is still much too wet. This area should be rebedded immediately to help with the drying process. Unfortunately, the water has to dissipate from underneath, so it all depends on how the subsoil will handle it. You could dig down about a foot and add a gravel layer, if necessary. I suggest you wait until March or so, after the spring thaw, to see how the ground is then."

"It is a shame that this has happened," Burrows said, as he bent down to pick away some muddy broken leaves. 'The meadowsweet was planted nearly two hundred years ago by the original owner, Samuel Barkeley, and supposedly came from Elizabeth the First's own gardens. She favored this above all fragrances for her rooms."

"There was wild sienna, too, and pineapple sage," Jed said, remembering the old yellowed drawings of the garden his father had once showed him. "This side is the fragrance side." He turned and pointed to the opposite 'leaf' of the fleur-de-lis. "And that's the culinary side. The top 'leaf' is the medicinal section."

"Your memory is excellent, sir," Burrows said, nodding his head. "Miss Rachel will be happy to know that there is some hope here. I'll advise the gardening service of your recommendations."

Jed smiled. "Tell you what, since I'm here, I'll reshape the bed for you. If it's enough, then you can replant next spring. Fortunately, you have enough of the same plants left on either side of the damaged area to divide and propagate. They could use a little thinning, too; they're too wild-looking. This time next year, you'll never know the bed had been damaged."

Burrows nearly beamed in pleasure. "Thank you, sir. This is most kind of you. Most kind. As a small measure of payment, I shall prepare shirred eggs and blueberry muffins for breakfast."

"You sure know how to feed a kidnap victim," Jed replied, grinning. "Does the little shed behind the garage still house the gardening things?"

"Yes, sir."

"Then I'll get started."

He waited until Burrows was back in the house before walking slowly around the rest of the herb garden. Unfortunately, volunteering to fix the garden was hardly the help Rae needed from him, he realized, but it helped him avoid something else.

Although he'd told her the situation wasn't hopeless, and it wasn't, he knew he wasn't ready to accept that the answer to the alternate site wasn't to be found in the reports. They'd been sorted every which way and still nothing promising had turned up. The answer lay elsewhere, but that meant leaving the estate and Rae. It was the last thing he wanted to do. He hated the thought of not seeing her for days, not making love with her and waking up to find her sleeping next to him. He found such immense satisfaction in that. A day without her presence would be unbearable.

Jed stopped in his tracks. His jaw dropped in astonishment as he realized why being with Rae was more important than a job.

He was in love with her.

It was why he'd been fighting for her, risking his career to keep the home she loved. It explained his obvious behavior. It was so damned obvious now.

He started laughing, as he thought of the butler's words. Burrows had known all along. Hell, he thought in amusement, while remembering his own reasoning that it had been the house causing his obvious behavior. How wrong could a person be? Then he remembered something else and his mirth faded.

Glancing up at Rae's bedroom window, he wondered if her behavior had been as obvious as his. Burrows *had* included her in his observation. The man might not have a green thumb for gardening, but Jed doubted the butler was often wrong in

his judgment of people. Rae probably hadn't recognized her own symptoms yet.

Maybe he ought to tell her. . . .

Jed grinned to himself, deciding to wait until
she realized it herself.

He couldn't wait to see the expression on her
face when she did.

Twelve

Rae tugged her robe tighter around her and sighed, as she watched Jed from her bedroom window.

What, she wondered, was she going to do with him? He was supposed to be fixing up a new site for the marina complex, and instead, he was fixing up the herb garden.

The better question, she decided, was what she was going to do with herself. She'd always been a fairly sensible woman. Well, at least until Jed had reentered her life, she amended with a wry smile. Since then, she'd been in a state of confusion.

Yesterday morning, she'd been too angry to think rationally. Now that she was calmer, she realized Henry Morrison's words were just that—words. She honestly couldn't say that they were true. It was just that she'd been vulnerable to the jolt Morrison delivered.

If only she were more sure of Jed, she thought. Their relationship was so fragile that it had seemed easier to believe the worst of him. There were times when he was still the Jed she remembered so well, and times when he seemed like a total stranger. She imagined there were moments when he had found her completely different from the girl he'd known. They had both grown up, and she had fallen in love. She just needed reassurance that she wasn't misplacing her heart.

Silently, she admitted that she had to give him a chance—she had to trust him. She knew love and trust were intertwined; she couldn't offer one without offering the other. Their relationship was so new and fragile that it could also be easily shattered. She *had* to believe that Jed hadn't lied to her about searching for a new complex site. She *had* to believe Henry Morrison was wrong about Jed. She *had* to have faith in him . . . and in her heart.

But what the hell was he doing in the damn garden?

"Ah! You are up, miss. Good morning."

Rae turned around as Burrows entered the bedroom. He carried a fully loaded coffee tray. Setting it down on the walnut table next to the window, he poured her a cup and offered it to her.

"You're spoiling me," she said, as she accepted it and took a reviving sip of the steaming black brew.

He nearly smiled. "Thank you, miss. It's agreeable to know that I am performing my duties well."

She chuckled.

"Mr. Jed has offered to repair some of the damage in the herb garden," he went on, "and if I may say so, I am relieved. He has more knowledge of what's needed than that . . ." His lips tightened for a moment. "That so-called gardening service."

"So I noticed," she said dryly, while pointing out of the window.

"You don't sound happy, miss."

"Believe me, Burrows, I'm thrilled down to my toes."

The butler drew himself up and glared at her. "You should be thankful for Mr. Jed's able assistance."

She felt her cheeks heating at the deserved reprimand. "I'm sorry. It's just that . . . I don't know if his behavior is as obvious as mine."

"So he has told you about my observation," Burrows said.

"He thinks the house is possessed and making everyone act crazy," she said, turning back to look out the window.

She heard a suspicious snort that reminded her of suppressed laughter, and she turned around again. Burrows's face was red, and his jaw was tensed in an obvious attempt to keep from venting his amusement. Helplessly, she began to giggle.

"He's something, isn't he?" she asked, shaking her head.

"Yes, miss, he is, and if I may say so, very well suited to you."

Her mirth instantly subsided, and she set the coffee cup on the table and returned her gaze to the window. "I know he's well-suited, Burrows."

"That is what you are not happy with, isn't it, miss?"

"I'm . . . unsure."

"If it were a choice between this estate and Mr. Jed, which would you choose?"

For a long minute, she watched Jed set boards around the damaged section. Finally she smiled sadly and said, "I'd like to think I have a choice to make, Burrows."

Four hours later, Rae found herself being hustled into Jed's BMW sports car.

"Are you crazy?" she asked, after he had tossed a hamper full of food in the back and had settled into the driver's seat. "It's barely fifty out here, and you want to have a picnic lunch in the park?"

The car roared to life, and he nearly shouted over the engine's whine, "Sounds great to me."

"I'll remind you of that later, when your buns are frozen."

He laughed. "You can always warm them up."

"Sex maniac," she muttered, shaking her head.

"What?"

"Never mind." She waved a hand. "Lead on, Waters. At least we won't have to worry about ants."

Lapsing into silence, she decided he had one heck of a work schedule. He'd spent the entire morning on the garden, and now was taking an afternoon picnic. It was disheartening to know that he wasn't even making a pretense of looking for a new site.

Pushing the thought away, she reminded herself about giving him a chance. It wasn't fair to condemn him on circumstantial evidence. She vowed not to allow her doubts to interfere any longer, and she would start right now by enjoying the picnic lunch. Suppressing a groan, she admitted she might not be a candidate for Resident Eccentric, but Jed certainly was.

It was a short drive over the bridge to the park, and after finding a suitable spot under the trees, they started eating the lunch Burrows had packed.

"Still think it's too cold?" Jed asked later as they lounged on a thick horse blanket and nibbled at the remains of their meal.

"I'm wearing a heating pad under my jeans," she replied, before popping a cracker into her mouth.

He chuckled, then sipped his glass of wine. The air was brisker than he had thought. Still, there was a beautiful pink glow in Rae's cheeks. "At least we didn't have to bother chilling the wine."

"Or the caviar. No crowds either."

"Do people use this park much in the summer?" he asked, curious. The park was deserted again, as it had been when they came with the boys. Of course, it was October.

"I don't think so. At least I've never seen more than a dozen people here at any one time." She grinned. "It seems like the Barkeley Club uses it more than anyone else."

Jed grinned in return. "Still looking for that treasure, right?"

She leaned back on her elbows and laughed. "I have the feeling they'll never give up now."

With hooded eyes, he admired the slender line of her thighs and the tilt of her breasts under the jacket she wore. A deep satisfaction ran through him at the thought that he could touch her at any time, and she would respond. Her happiness mattered very much to him, and he would do everything in his power to give her what she wanted.

He resisted the sudden urge to tell her what Burrows had actually meant. She deserved the time to discover it on her own.

He finished his wine, then stood up and held out a hand to her. "Come on. We can clean up later. Let's take a walk around."

Smiling, she accepted his offer, and he helped her to her feet. They walked hand in hand along the paths through the dense woods by the riverbank.

"Both of us should be working," Rae finally said, as they stopped to untangle several strands of her hair from a low tree branch.

"Do you want to go back?"

She chuckled. "No. I just thought I'd point out the obvious."

"A lunch break never hurt anyone. You hibernated in that library all morning."

"That's my busiest time, between the clients calling and Wall Street opening. Just before closing it gets hectic again."

"I promise to have you back by three."

They strolled along for a few more moments, before she said, "I was surprised to see you working in the garden this morning."

"Burrows was upset about the damage, so I thought I'd help out. It's been years since I've done that kind of work, but I've got to admit I enjoyed it." He glanced at her. "Why?"

She shrugged. "Just surprised."

"I hear the implied reprimand, Madam," he said, patting her cheek. "I'll have you know I'm working very hard on finding another site. Can't you tell?"

"You are bad, Jed," she said, shaking her head.

He grinned at her. "Yeah, I know. But you like it."

"Wise guy," she murmured.

Chuckling, he shifted his gaze to the quiet grounds of the park. He hadn't actually lied. While he'd been working in the garden, he'd found his eyes straying more and more to the wooded area on the other side of the river. A crazy idea had occurred to him, and he'd decided to at least take a look about the park. A picnic with Rae seemed the perfect way to do so. In fact, anywhere with her was the perfect way to spend a day. Or night. . .

Nearly tripping over a tree root reminded him to concentrate on what he knew about the park, which wasn't much. It hadn't been in the site reports, and he had to admit that was a bad sign. Unfortunately, he couldn't remember whether the park had even been looked at by the company. Maybe someone had only given it a cursory check. After all, the Barkeley estate had seemed like a sure thing.

Jed frowned to himself, as they continued their stroll. He'd been hoping to see some homes within the boundaries, which would have meant the park was zoned for residential buildings. There weren't any. He didn't even know whether the park was a federal, state, or county one, and that would make a big difference. There were probably other obstacles to consider too. Still, if they could be solved, the park would be perfect for the marina complex. It had all the qualities of the estate plus one more. He couldn't think of a grander view than the elegant grounds of the Barkeley home.

Absently pulling a leaf from a leggy growth of bush, he wondered if he should tell her about his idea. Not yet, he thought. After all, the park was only a nebulous possibility at the moment. He would make several calls after they returned to the house.

"Jed!" Rae suddenly exclaimed, breaking into his thoughts. "Are you holding what I think you're holding?"

He looked down at the sprig he'd been lazily twirling between his fingers . . . and instantly dropped it. "Dammit! Poison oak!"

"Really?" Rae bent down to examine it. "I thought it was poison ivy."

"Good thing you knew it was poison something," he said, silently cursing the fact that there was no soap and water handy. "Let's just hope it's too late in the season for us to be affected by it."

"Us?" she drawled, as she straightened and arched an eyebrow.

"Us," he said firmly. "Because there's no way I'm moving back to that damn trophy room."

"That's what I was afraid of," she muttered,

rubbing her hand against his possibly affected one. "Might as well get it now, and get it over with."

Jed shook his head. "My way would have been more fun."

She grinned. "I'm sure we'll find a new use for calamine lotion."

He burst into laughter.

Later that evening, Jed stared out the kitchen window at the park. He had made his phone calls, and one had turned up a piece of good news. His assistants hadn't done more than a cursory check of the park, since the company had expected to acquire the estate. What the other phone calls would turn up was a huge guess. He crossed his fingers that his would be the correct one.

"That's the fourth time you've stared out that window," Rae commented, as she dished up ice cream for them. "What's so interesting out there?"

"Just enjoying the view," he said with a grin.

On Friday night, Rae admitted defeat.

As she paced her bedroom, she muttered curses under her breath. All of them were directed at Jed.

Over the past three days, he had done everything *but* work on the new site. Oh sure, there had been telephone calls for him, she told herself, but that was the extent of it. He'd spent the mornings in the library with her, asking questions about her work. She appreciated his interest. Really she did. He had helped Burrows polish silver on Wednesday afternoon, and rearranged the drawing room on Thursday. He'd also "tsked-tsked" the condition of the grounds with the butler until the two of them were happy as clams. And when he wasn't busy with other things, he'd succeeded in enticing her into bed. She conceded she hadn't put up much resistance about those "work breaks."

It was time to face the truth, she thought. He was no longer looking for a new site. But why? Every time she'd hinted he ought to be working, he would just reply that it was "under control." It was almost as if he'd been avoiding it. . . .

Her eyes widened, and she halted her pacing. He'd been hard at it Monday, but after that he'd made no effort on the project. Something must have happened between those two days, and she had a pretty good idea what it was. Morrison's phone call. Maybe Jed had been told to stop work on a new site, and maybe Morrison had been the one to tell him.

"Stop it!" she hissed to herself, while covering her face with her hands.

She wasn't being fair again, and she knew it. She also knew she couldn't continue on the way she was. She had to corner Jed and get the answers she so badly needed. It was what she should have done in the first place.

She lowered her hands when she heard footsteps in the hallway.

"All locked up," Jed said, as he entered the bedroom. The dogs rushed past him into the room. He frowned at them and pointed to the door. "Out! You guys are supposed to be roaming the halls in case of burglars."

Rae watched in amazement, as both dogs reluctantly left the room. She could understand Samson obeying him, but not Delilah. "Since when did you make friends with Delilah?"

Shutting the door, he chuckled. "I'm as surprised as you are that she listened. I think I'm growing on her."

As he strode across the room, she braced herself to confront him, but before she could say a word, his mouth settled firmly on hers.

She was startled for a moment, then her insides melted as he pressed her against his hard body. Her arms crept up around his neck. When he finally lifted his head, she gave a long sigh.

He kissed her lightly on the nose and whispered, "You know how to make a man feel good."

"You know how to make a woman feel good," she murmured back, resting her head on his chest. She knew she ought to ask him about the site, but decided a few more minutes wouldn't hurt.

"You never did settle on my ransom," he murmured, caressing her back with his strong hands.

"I'm thinking of keeping you," she said softly. "Jed—"

He hushed her with another kiss. "I'd love to stay forever, but I have to take a leave of absence on Monday."

Her head snapped up. "What?"

"There are some people I need to see, Rae," he said, taking her arms from around his neck and stepping out of the embrace. Still holding her right hand, he began to walk toward the bed. "Let's sit down and—"

She refused to budge, and he stopped to gaze at

her with puzzled eyes. "No. Let's stand up. Why are you leaving?"

He frowned. "I told you. I have to see some people on Monday, and I should go in to the office. I've been ignoring my other work for the new site—"

"I see." She pulled her hand from his. Her whole body felt ice cold at the announcement of his unexpected departure. Maybe it wasn't so unexpected, she thought numbly. Maybe she had been forcing herself to ignore the truth. Henry Morrison had given her fair warning. "Well, I shouldn't be surprised, should I, Jed? I should have known Morrison was right."

"What are you talking about?" he asked.

She drew in an uninterrupted breath. "I'm talking about how convenient it is to suddenly have people you need to talk to, and other work to do. What happened to the work on the new site?"

"Nothing—"

"That's what I thought," she broke in. "Your boss made it very clear to me on Monday that he wants the estate. He also made it very clear that you always get him what he wants."

"What?" he exclaimed, staring at her in puzzlement. "Henry talked to you?"

"Oh, yes." She smiled grimly. "And he had quite a lot to say."

"Why," he gritted between clenched teeth, "didn't you tell me he talked to you?"

"Because it was a very interesting conversation, Jed." Her smile felt frozen now. Maybe he hadn't known about the conversation, but he still worked for Morrison. She had forgotten that all too often lately. His leaving now, and with such a flimsy excuse, proved that. She went on. "I think the thing that stood out the most was that your real job has been to talk me into selling to Atlantic—in any way possible."

"You believed him?"

"Yes, at first," she admitted, folding her arms across her chest. "Then I decided I wasn't being fair not to trust you. So I gave you a chance to prove my trust wasn't misplaced. You've certainly done that this past week."

"What chance, Rae?" he asked angrily. "You give me a lousy deadline that I don't even know about to prove something in your damn mind because of a stupid phone call you don't tell me about, and you call that trusting me?"

"I thought that actions would speak louder than words." Her voice cracked for an instant. She inhaled, then added, "I was wrong."

He glared at her. The fury in his hazel eyes was easy to read. "Dammit, Rae! The man says something totally stupid and out of line, and you believe him rather than me."

"What was I supposed to believe?" she snapped, feeling the tears push against her eyelids. "That you've been actively looking for another site? You never meant to find one, did you? You were just stringing me along until I was pliable, weren't you? You've been playing on my . . . emotions, and now this 'leave of absence' is just your way of easing out gracefully while I still trust you. I've known all along what you've been up to, Jed, and your boss only confirmed it!"

He brushed past her and strode toward the door. After opening it, he turned around. "Don't be so self-righteous, Rae. You hopped into my bed fast enough. What were you after? Sex with the gardener's boy?"

He couldn't have hurt her more if he had slapped her in the face. She stared at him, then lifted her chin and lied.

"Yes."

He slammed the door behind him.

Thirteen

Tuesday morning, Jed walked very calmly into Henry Morrison's office and dropped a pile of papers on the desk.

"Here's your damn site," he said coldly. "Cheaper and better than the Barkeley estate ever would have been. By the way, I quit."

"Jed!"

He turned around and strode out the door.

"If I may say so, miss, you have surpassed Mr. Merriman for foolish stubbornness."

"Burrows, please," Rae murmured, continuing to gaze at the stock market quotes on her computer screen.

"Going to your house in New York for nearly two weeks," he continued, ignoring her, "and never a word . . ."

She let his voice drone on, rather than bother

telling him she'd already lectured herself sick. Besides, it would take more energy than she possessed to try and dissuade him. The only good thing about her time in the city was that she had regained enough control to function like a robot.

Almost from the moment Jed had stormed out of her house, she had known she was wrong. She had hurt him terribly. At the thought of his "leave of absence," she turned all her fears into accusations, and he retaliated with one of his own.

Feeling her throat begin to tighten, she swallowed in an attempt to quell the feeling.

Just as she had been unjustified, so had he. Her pride and her pain had been riding her like twin devils by the time she realized that. Foolish stubbornness, Burrows had called it, and he was right. With one little word, she *had* been very foolish and very stubborn. If she had only answered him differently when he accused her of just having sex with him, he never would have walked out the door. But she hadn't, and he had. . . .

The telephone rang, cutting off her thoughts and Burrows's words.

Grateful for the interruption, Rae grabbed for the receiver before the butler could. Hoping against hope that it would be Jed, she picked it up.

"Hello?" she said, giving Burrows a tiny smile of false apology.

"Rachel? Is that you?"

The voice was very faint, but all too familiar. In shock, she exclaimed, "Uncle Merry! Where . . . Are you still in Nepal?"

"Where else would I be, dear child?"

"I mean . . . I thought there wasn't a phone at the monastery," she sputtered, astonished to hear his voice.

"There isn't. But it would seem things do change in fifty years. The government finally installed a line to the village headman's house last year. I just thought I would call to let you know that I arrived safe and sound."

"Do you know all the trouble you've caused?" she nearly shouted, as she realized that she could finally vent her anger on the proper person. "That business with Atlantic Developers—"

"Calm down, dear child. It was just a little mix-up."

"Hardly!"

"Really? The lawyers should have had it straightened out by now. I can't see any reason for a hullabaloo. Surely with Jed handling the transaction for his company . . ."

To Rae's surprise, she suddenly felt fat tears rolling down her cheeks. She tried unsuccessfully to gulp them back and muttered, "Dammit, Merry."

"I beg pardon, but did you say something? There's some static on the line."

A sudden crackling reached her ears. She sniffled and raised her voice. "I said, 'dammit'!"

"Are you crying, child?"

"Yes, I'm crying."

Burrows thrust a handkerchief under her nose. She took it and wiped her eyes. "First, you made a mess, then I made a mess. Jed—"

"How is the lad?" Merriman asked, breaking in.

She caught back a sob. "I don't know."

"What the hell do you mean you don't know?"

he demanded from halfway across the world. "Haven't you seen him? Talked to him?"

"I'm trying to tell you about it!"

"Oh."

Taking a deep breath, Rae informed her uncle of everything that had happened since he'd left for his retirement. She didn't spare herself. As a last note, she added, "I was a fool, Uncle Merry. A complete and total fool. Much as I would love to blame you for starting it all, I was the one who lost Jed."

"I don't under . . . Where was Burrows during all this—"

"What does Burrows have to do with it?" she asked, glancing in confusion at the stone-faced butler. "Believe me, I didn't need any help messing up my life."

"Well, of course. I just meant that Burrows is usually a wealth of information on matters of the heart. He's a pain in the rear end, but I do have to admit that he does have a romantic nature." Rae stared at the subject in question, trying to find a Joan Wilder under the butler's stoic exterior. "If you had gone to him, he might have given you the benefit of his insight."

"He did try," Rae admitted, remembering Burrows's observations. "But I had my own stupid ideas."

"I'm sure all is not lost, Rachel." Merriman chuckled. "What you need to do is to regain some of your Barkeley backbone. Just go after Jed and beg his forgiveness. It's easy."

"But I said the most horrible things to him—"

"In the heat of the moment, dear child. You

can't be held responsible for your actions. I'm sure he'll forgive you."

She didn't bother to tell her uncle how many times she had picked up the phone to apologize to Jed, and how each time she'd hung up before dialing. She knew no apology would outweigh her accusations.

"It's not that easy," she began, while wiping away fresh tears. Lord, she thought, she'd never felt so emotionally drained.

"You'll work it all out, dear child," her uncle said optimistically. "The temple bell is ringing to call the monks in to prayer, so I must go. If Burrows is handy, might I speak with him for a moment?"

"Of course."

She handed the receiver to Burrows, and needing to be alone, she got up from her chair and left the room. She wandered across the hall and into the drawing room. Even though the furniture had been rearranged, memories of the night she and Jed had made love for the first time flooded her mind.

Spinning on her heel, she tried to think of a room that wouldn't haunt her with some image of Jed, and realized there was none. It had been a mistake to come back to the estate, she thought. Since she'd arrived yesterday, she had been constantly reminded of Jed. There wasn't a place she could go without feeling pain and guilt stabbing at her.

With a silent curse, she tightened her hands into fists. Damn this house! It had always been the obstacle between them. She had been fighting for her heritage, and Jed had been fighting for his career. Now the house would always be a symbol of what she had won . . . and lost.

She couldn't go on like this, she thought frantically, as a kind of blind panic welled up inside her. There had to be something she could do that would get him back, and it had to be something so perfect that he would know that she did love him . . . and did trust him. Something that would absolutely and totally convince him . . .

She nearly jumped out of her own skin when she realized exactly what that something was.

"There you are, miss," Burrows said, coming out of the library. "I—"

"Did Uncle Merry finally hang up?" she asked, rushing past him into the room.

"Yes, miss."

"Great. I have a very important call to make."

"It is good of you to receive me, sir," Burrows said.

Jed hesitated for a bare instant, then took the butler's hand and shook it. "It's good to see you again. Please sit down."

Nodding, Burrows perched himself on the sofa. Jed took a seat across from him in a stuffed rocker and smiled as the older man looked around the living room. He admitted that his furnished condominium was more a place to hang his suit jacket, and it looked it.

"Would you like a drink?" Jed asked. "Coffee? Tea?"

"No, thank you, sir," Burrows said. "I have come about Miss Rachel, sir."

"That wasn't hard to figure out," Jed said, leaning back in the rocker. What he couldn't figure out was why he had even agreed to see the man in the first place. Every time he'd thought of Rae pain had festered, and he wanted it to keep festering. Maybe that was why, he thought. There was a perverse pleasure in just hearing about her.

Nodding, Burrows cleared his throat. "Before I say anything further, I must request that she never be told of this conversation. She has no idea I have come to see you, and, frankly, sir, I am committing a horrible breach of etiquette. But I felt it was extremely important."

Jed dipped his head once to show his agreement to the request.

Burrows continued. "Although a butler is not supposed, in essence, to see or hear anything of his employer's personal life, I am aware that there has been a rift between you and Miss Rachel."

"And?" Jed said impatiently. If Burrows thought he was going to make some kind of reconciliation, he was wasting his breath.

"I readily admit that whatever has occurred is your business and hers. I have no wish to interfere there. However, Miss Rachel has done something that I think is also your business—"

"Is she pregnant?" Jed demanded, sitting upright. The thought had come from nowhere, but now it left a hollowness in the pit of his stomach. "You said she did something. My God! She didn't—?"

"No!" Burrows exclaimed vehemently, clearly understanding. "No, sir, nothing like that. I have no idea if she is even . . . with child."

Jed felt relief and disappointment run through him at the same time. Suddenly restless, he left the chair and began pacing the living room. "Well?"

"What I was attempting to say, sir, is that I feel you have a right to know that she placed the estate in the hands of a realtor, two days ago."

Stunned, Jed turned in midstride. "Placed the . . . she's selling the house?"

Burrows nodded. "Yes, sir."

"After all I went through to save it for her!" Jed half shouted, slamming a fist into the nearest object—a floor lamp. He ignored it as it crashed to the ground. "She can't do that! Dammit, it was . . . she only cared . . . what the hell . . . !" Realizing how incoherent he sounded, he returned to the rocker and flopped down in it. "But why would she do that? She loves that place. Why, Burrows?"

"That is the oddest part, sir. She won't say why. She is very willful and determined, though."

"But what about you?" Jed asked, as the question suddenly came to him. "And the dogs? And Harvey? What about all of you?"

"She says we shall all move back to her house in New York." Burrows gave a tiny shudder. "I am fond of a quiet life, but I will not leave her service now. I suspect the dogs and the spider will adjust more easily than I shall. Dogs are happy anywhere, so long as they have their master's affection. I doubt the spider will care."

"Have there been any offers for the place?" Jed asked almost absently, as his mind churned with confusion. "Was Atlantic one of the calls?"

"I could not say, not being privy to whom the realtor had interested in the estate. I have managed to put them off, so far. I don't think Miss Rachel has realized that she hasn't answered the telephone in two days. I would have come sooner, but I had to wait until she was out of the house. She is visiting her mother this afternoon." Ruefully, Burrows shook his head. "I am hoping, sir, that you can do something to stop her."

Jed pressed his fingers to his temples and muttered, "I need to think."

She was selling the estate. The words ran through his mind like a litany. She had defended her home against him. She hadn't trusted him with it. Now, when everything was over, she was selling. Why? Why now?

He had worked like a madman to prevent the deal with the estate from ever entering Henry Morrison's head again. Even if Henry had heard it was suddenly on the market, he doubted if his former boss would touch it now. It would appeal to Henry's nature to have the complex sitting right across the river from the Barkeley home.

After storming out of her house, he had spent the weekend tracking down the right people in an effort to investigate and secure the park as the new site. He had done it, too. A small portion of the park had been rezoned shortly after Atlantic's first inquiry months ago. It seemed that the company's interest—however short-lived—had spurred the county government to reconsider the opportunity for additional revenues. He negotiated a terrific deal and dropped it all on Henry's desk, along with his resignation. Henry had begged him to

come back, too, and there had been other job
offers. Gratifying as they were, he had never felt
so damned self-righteous in his life as he had at
having proved Rae wrong. He'd been living on the
feeling ever since.

There had been times, though, during the past
several weeks, when he began to wonder if he'd
asked too much of her, but he immediately suppressed the thoughts. All she had ever cared about
was the estate, and she had made that painfully
clear.

Now she was selling. Why give up the only thing
she had wanted all along? Obviously, something
had happened to cause her change of heart. . . .

Jed jumped out of the chair and demanded,
"Burrows, does Rae know that Atlantic bought
the park property?"

"The park? The one on the other side of the
river?"

"Yes, that one."

The butler swallowed visibly. "Your condominium complex will be right across from the estate?"

Jed nodded, hoping the answer was the one he
needed.

"Heaven forbid," Burrows muttered, closing his
eyes. He opened them. "Since I did not know, I
doubt very much that Miss Rachel does."

So she wasn't selling because of the view, Jed
thought, as a huge grin spread across his features. For all she knew, she was opening herself
to lawsuits galore from Atlantic. Although Burrows claimed to have come in secret, Rae must
have been aware that Jed would eventually hear
about the sale. In fact, he'd bet his last dime on

it. The sale was her way of saying that she loved him. What it must have cost her to do such a thing! Actions did speak louder than words, he decided. They could say quite a lot.

"You say she's at her mother's?" Jed asked, as he mulled over several actions he could take. Whatever he did, it would have to be damn good to match hers.

"Yes, sir." Burrows stood up. "This all means something to you, doesn't it?"

Jed laughed. "Obvious behavior, Burrows. Now I have to be just as obvious, and I'll need your help."

"Alicia must have misunderstood the boys," Vivian Barkeley said, as she walked arm in arm with her daughter to the front door.

"I don't know where they get these things," Rae replied with a straight face. "Me kidnap some man?"

"I told Alicia the same thing, dear." Her mother opened the heavy oak door. "But you know Alicia; she's very excitable."

Her sister-in-law was a pain in the tush, Rae thought, stepping out onto the front patio of the sprawling Main Line house. Alicia was a gossipy snob, but Rae cursed herself for not swearing her nephews to secrecy. Still, her mother didn't have to know.

"Why don't you come over for lunch on Sunday, Mom?" she asked, turning to face her mother.

Before Vivian could answer, a car roared up the

U-shaped drive and screeched to a halt in front of the house. It was the antique Rolls.

Rae stared in amazement as Jed scrambled out of the front passenger seat. Fearing something horrible must have happened, she ran to him. "Did something happen? Is someone hurt?"

"Nope." He grinned at her, resting one arm on the top of the open car door. "But you're about to be kidnapped."

"Kidnapped!" Rae and her mother exclaimed at the same moment.

Before Rae could move, he reached out and very calmly hoisted her up onto his shoulder. Shocked and disoriented, Rae suddenly found herself with a bird's-eye view of his rear.

She braced her hands on his backside and pushed herself up enough to angle her head. "You can't be serious, Jed! Now what is this really all about?"

"I just told you," he said. "Mrs. Barkeley, would you like to see your daughter get married?"

"Married!" Both women exclaimed again.

"I'm kidnapping your daughter and taking her to Maryland to get married."

"What!" It was all happening too fast, Rae realized dimly. Her heart was swelling with joy, but her mind was telling her it could be some kind of revenge. She blocked out the thought.

"Trust me, Mrs. Barkeley, your daughter is only going to get married once. To me."

"But . . . but!" Rae heard her mother's voice stutter.

"I don't think you should leave any witnesses, Mr. Jed." Burrows's voice magically materialized.

"I'm afraid Mrs. Barkeley will have to accompany us. It's quite all right, madam. Mr. Jed is most sincere, however unorthodox his methods."

"Burrows, what the hell are you doing?" Rae shouted, twisting and turning to try and find the butler. Dammit, she thought. He could have told her, at least!

"I am driving the getaway car, miss."

"Burrows!"

"Well, if I'm going to be abducted, too, I should get my coat," Vivian said matter-of-factly.

"Mom!" If she didn't know better, Rae would have sworn her mother was a conspirator.

"I'll have to escort you into the house, madam, to insure you don't call the police," Burrows said.

"Oh! I never thought of that."

"Great," Rae muttered, dropping her head against Jed's hip. "I'm being kidnapped, and my own mother doesn't even think to call the police."

She grinned to herself.

"Your mom's going to make a great mother-in-law," Jed commented. He opened the rear car door, then bending low, he gently tipped her onto the seat.

Finally able to see his face, she searched his features. His hazel eyes were gleaming with delight and mischief. His mustache quivered as he tried to keep a smile from his lips.

"You're enjoying this."

He finally grinned. "Damn right."

She lowered her eyes for a moment, then lifted them. "I love you, Jed."

"Hell of a way to tell me," he said, taking her in his arms. "Putting the estate up for sale like that."

"The house is important to me," she said, holding his gaze. "But it's up to you what happens to it. I'd rather be with you wherever you are, than be in the house without you."

He swallowed visibly. "I could say you should sell it to Atlantic."

She nodded slowly. "I know. I trust you, Jed."

His mouth covered hers fiercely, and she melted against him. She wrapped her arms around him, joyfully giving herself up to the kiss.

"I hurt you," she murmured, when he finally lifted his head. "I'll spend the rest of my life making it up to you."

"Hush," he whispered against her lips. "We hurt each other, and we'll spend the rest of *our* lives making it up. On the estate."

She hugged him. "Our estate."

"By the way, you're marrying a bum. I quit my job."

"What!" She pushed at his shoulders so she could see his face.

He nodded. "I think I did it because it came between us, although at the time I didn't see it."

"You just go right back and get it, Jedidiah Waters!" she ordered. "You worked too hard to give it up now."

"I suppose I should be employed," he said, then laughed. "Henry's been after me to come back ever since I left."

"Good. Now there's one more thing we have to straighten out," she said, and kissed him. "You could have *asked* me to marry you. Believe me, Jed, it beats worrying about the rap for kidnapping, if you're caught."

He chuckled. "Actions speak louder than words. Besides, I was taking no chances with you."

She burst into laughter.

When she sobered, he kissed her again. There was a long silence in the car.

"Why are we going to Maryland to get married?" she finally asked.

He grinned. "It's the quickest way to get you married to me. Only a two-day waiting period."

She made a face. "Still much too long."

"Ahem!"

Startled, they both glanced around to find Vivian Barkeley standing next to the car.

"None of that until after the wedding."

Sighing in unison, they untangled themselves and sat up. Her mother shut the door. Burrows helped Vivian into the front.

"I must say, you're taking this very well, Mom," Rae complained.

"Burrows has explained that this is for your own good, Rachel," Vivian said, turning around. "I will speak to you later about your lying to me this afternoon. It seems my grandsons knew exactly what they were talking about. You're becoming as outrageous as Merriman, dear."

"Not outrageous, Mom. Obvious." Rae smiled at Jed.

"And it had better stay that way," he whispered in her ear.

Epilogue

Rae moved slowly around the herb garden, as the first waves of June's summer heat beat down on her. She wiped the perspiration from her forehead and tried to ignore the noise of the heavy construction taking place directly across the river.

"Some wedding present," she muttered under her breath, as she clipped fresh chervil from the thriving plants.

Jed had saved that little piece of news until after the wedding. At the time, she hadn't been sure whether to kiss him or strangle him. Since the construction had begun, she was quite sure. She should have strangled him.

"Dammit, Rae! You know what the doctor said!"

Straightening with a groan, she watched her husband stride across the back lawn. "You are supposed to be at the office!"

"I stopped at the site, and it was a damned good thing I did." Reaching her, he took the basket out of her hands. "I saw you from across the river. It can't be good for you, bending and straightening like that."

"Will you relax, Jed!" she said in exasperation, absently resting her hands on her rounded belly. "I'm having a baby, for goodness' sake! The doctor only said to be sensible about what I do. Cutting herbs is hardly the decathlon."

"This heat is sure to make you sick again," he said, concern evident in his hazel eyes. "And you were already sick this morning."

"If you don't knock off this mother hen bit, I'll throw up on your shoes," she vowed, as he put his arm around her.

He only laughed in answer.

"I love you," she murmured, sliding her arms around his trim waist.

Jed kissed her hair. "Not as much as I love you."

He held her tightly, and she marveled at how much his embrace could renew her. Like the garden, their love thrived on the complete trust they had in each other. The baby inside her kicked vigorously.

Jed chuckled indulgently. "Definitely a candidate for the Barkeley Club."

"The Waters Club," Rae corrected, snuggling as close to him as her six-month pregnancy would allow.

Across the river, the lunch whistle sounded, drawing their attention. Keeping an arm around each other, they looked across to the site.

"Isn't it looking great?" Jed asked proudly as he

gazed at the steel girders thrusting up out of the ground.

"Great," Rae said dryly.

"Well, I see I've missed the wedding!"

Startled, both of them turned around at the sound of the voice. Rae's mouth dropped open in complete astonishment, as Merriman Barkeley smiled cheerfully at her. Tall, with silvery-dark hair, her uncle was elegantly dressed in a white suit. He also had his arms around two very young, very beautiful women, who walked on either side of him, as he made his way down the garden path.

"Uncle Merry! What are you doing here?" Rae asked, as her initial shock wore off. She hurried over to receive his exuberant hug.

"All in good time, dear child," he said, chuckling. "First, I see everything worked out with Jed. And very well."

"No thanks to you," she said tartly, then grinned.

"Jed, my boy!" Merriman exclaimed, as Jed joined them. "Welcome to the family."

"You old reprobate. How are you?" Jed laughed and shook hands with the older man. Rae stepped back to her husband's side, and he put his arm around her waist again.

"I've never been fitter, my boy! Oh, children, let me introduce you to Nadine and Michelle. They don't speak a word of English. Only French."

The women smiled at the mention of their names. Smiling back, Rae murmured to Merriman. "Now why *don't* I think you found them at a monastery?"

"Must have been one hell of a prayer," Jed muttered, smiling at the women.

"Well, I did say a few grateful prayers after I met up with the girls," Merriman admitted. "At my age, I had to."

Giggling, Rae shook her head.

"What is this, Mr. Merriman?" Burrows demanded, striding toward the group.

"Burrows!" Merriman waved happily at him. "I was wondering where you were hiding."

"I was in the house preparing lunch. I ask you again, sir, what is this?"

Merriman winked at Rae, then said, "I came back for the wedding, of course, and I brought Nadine for you, old fellow."

He indicated the girl on his right, who smiled brilliantly at the butler.

Rae couldn't stand it. She fell back into Jed's arms in a fit of laughter. Jed was laughing so hard that she thought they would both collapse onto the brick-lined path.

"Mr. Merriman!" Burrows said sternly. "I can find my own women, thank you very much!"

"You'll hurt the poor girl's feelings, Burrows—"

"Please!" Jed broke in, trying to control himself. "You've got a lot of explaining to do, Merriman."

"It's quite simple, my boy. As you have probably surmised, I never retired to a monastery." The old scoundrel smiled happily. "Thank goodness! Instead I have been relaxing under a Tahitian sun, where I met these two lovely creatures, while my little matchmaking attempt with you two took its course."

"Matchmaking!" Rae and Jed exclaimed.

"Of course." He waved an arm expansively. "I took one look at Jed, all grown up, and knew he'd be perfect for you, Rachel. You weren't getting any younger, you know. So I agreed to sell the house, then deeded it to you. In the ruckus, I figured you two would make contact." He jerked his head at Burrows. "Fortunately, my 'spy' here didn't screw things up too much."

"I beg to differ with you, sir," Burrows said, glowering at Merriman. "I brought them through it quite handily, in spite of the quagmire you created."

"Why you—" Rae turned to Jed. "Do you want to kill them, or should I?"

"We'll kill them together," Jed pronounced.

"Now, children." Smiling, Merriman wagged a finger at them. "You must admit I was quite right."

"He's got us there," Jed said, gazing at his wife.

Suddenly, Merriman pointed behind them. "Just what the hell is that?"

"The condominium complex," Rae said sweetly. "That's where it finally ended up."

"Beautiful, isn't it?" Jed asked.

"No, it is not beautiful!" Merriman bellowed in outrage. "I won't stand for this . . . this monstrosity in my backyard!"

"Whose backyard?" Rae asked, her voice dripping sugar.

"Well, of course, you're going to give me back the house now," Merriman said confidently. "I only deeded it over to you to get things rolling along."

Rae looked at Jed. Jed gazed back at her. They

smiled evilly and turned to the man who had wreaked so much havoc.

"No."

"What!" Merriman squawked. "It's my house! Mine! You have to give it back!"

To everyone's amazement, Burrows burst into raucous laughter.

"Well done!" he gasped out, tears beginning to stream down his cheeks. "Serves him right!"

"I suppose he could live in the trophy room," Jed conceded, grinning at Rae.

"It has been his home for many years," she admitted, winking at Jed. "And Harvey's been lonely."

"I'm not sleeping with any damn spider!"

"The trophy room or nothing," Rae said, shrugging. She turned back to her husband, and they walked slowly toward the house, leaving Merriman shouting curses behind them.

"By the way, I'm kidnapping you for lunch, my love," she said, rubbing her cheek against his shoulder. "Do you mind?"

Jed kissed her. "A pleasure, Mrs. Waters. As always."

THE EDITOR'S CORNER

One of the best "presents" I've received at Bantam is the help of the very talented and wonderfully enthusiastic Barbara Alpert, who has written the copy for the back cover of almost every LOVESWEPT romance since the first book. (In fact, only three in all this time haven't been written by Barbara, and I wrote those.) As usual, Barbara has done a superb job of showcasing all the books next month, and so I thought I would give you a sneak peek at her copy on the marvelous books you can expect to keep your holiday spirits high.

First, we are delighted to welcome a brand-new writer—and our first Canadian author—Judy Gill, with **HEAD OVER HEELS,** LOVESWEPT #228. "The sultry laughter and tantalizing aromas that wafted across the fence from next door were enough to make a grown man cry, Buck Halloran thought—or else climb eight-foot fences! But the renowned mountain climber was confined to a wheelchair, casts on one arm and one leg . . . how could he meet the woman behind the smoky voice, the temptress who was keeper of the goodies? . . . He had to touch her, searing her lips with kisses that seduced her heart and soul—and Darcy Gallagher surrendered to the potent magic of his embrace. But the handsome wanderer who whispered sexy promises to her across the hedge at midnight had his eyes on a higher mountain, a new adventure, while she yearned to make a home for children and the man she loved. Could they join their lives and somehow share the dreams that gave them joy?"

Sandra Brown has given us a memorable gift of love in **TIDINGS OF GREAT JOY,** LOVESWEPT #229. As Barbara describes it, "Ria Lavender hadn't planned on spending a passionate Christmas night in front of a roaring fire with Taylor Mackensie. But somehow the scents of pine tree, wood smoke, and male flesh produced a kind of spontaneous combustion inside her, and morning found the lovely architect lying on her silver fox coat beside the mayor-elect, a man she hardly knew. Ten weeks later she knew she was pregnant with Taylor's child . . . and insisted they had to marry. A marriage 'in name only,' she promised him. Taylor agreed to a wedding, but shocked Ria with his demand that they live together as husband and wife—in every way. She couldn't deny she wanted him, the lady-killer with the devil's grin, but

(continued)

there was danger in succumbing to the heat he roused—in falling for a man she couldn't keep."

Prepare yourself for a session of hearty laughter and richly warming emotion when you read Joan Elliott Pickart's **ILLUSIONS,** LOVESWEPT #230. Barbara teases you unmercifully with her summary of this one! "There was definitely a naked man asleep in Cassidy Cole's bathtub! With his ruggedly handsome face and 'kissin' lips,' Sagan Jones was a single woman's dream, and how could she resist a smooth-talking vagabond with roving hands who promised he'd stay only until his luggage caught up with him? Sagan had come to Cherokee, Arizona, after promising Cassidy's brother he'd check up on her. He'd flexed his muscles, smiled his heart-stopping smile, and won over everyone in town except her. . . . Sagan had spent years running from loneliness, and though his lips vowed endless pleasures, Cassidy knew he wasn't a man to put down roots. . . . Could she make him see that in a world full of mirages and dreams that died with day, her love was real and everlasting?"

Hagen strikes again in Kay Hooper's delightful **THE FALL OF LUCAS KENDRICK,** LOVESWEPT #231. As Barbara tells you, "Time was supposed to obscure memories, but when Kyle Griffon saw the sunlight glinting off Lucas Kendrick's hair, she knew she'd never stopped waiting for him. Ten years before, he'd awakened her woman's passion, and when he left without a word, her quicksilver laughter had turned to anger, and her rebel's heart to a wild flirtation with danger—anything to forget the pain of losing him. Now he was back, and he needed her help in a desperate plan— but did she dare revive the flame of desire that once had burned her?" Only Josh, Raven, Rafferty, a few other fictional characters, Kay, Barbara, and I know right now. Be sure that you're one of the first next month to get the answer!

You can have the wish you wish as you read this: another great love story from Iris Johansen who gives you **STAR LIGHT, STAR BRIGHT,** LOVESWEPT #232. "When the golden-haired rogue in the black leather jacket dodged a barrage of bullets to rescue her, Quenby Swenson thrilled . . . with fear and with excitement," says Barbara most accurately. "Gunner Nilsen had risked his life to save her, but when he promised to cherish her for a lifetime, she refused to believe him. And yet she knew somehow he'd

(continued)

never lie to her, never hurt her, never leave her—even though she hardly knew him at all. He shattered her serenity, rippled her waters, vowing to play her body like the strings of a harp . . . until he'd learned all the melodies inside her. Quenby felt her heart swell with yearning for the dreams Gunner wove with words and caresses. Did she dare surrender to this mysterious man of danger, the untamed lover who promised her their souls were entwined for all time?"

For one of the most original, whimsical, and moving romances ever, you can't beat **THE BARON**, LOVESWEPT #233 by Sally Goldenbaum. Barbara whets your appetite with this terrific description: "Disguised as a glittering contessa for a glamorous mystery weekend, Hallie Finnegan knew anything was possible—even being swept into the arms of a dashing baron! She'd never been intriguing before, never enchanted a worldly man who stunned her senses with hungry kisses beneath a full moon. Once the 'let's pretend mystery' was solved, though, they shed their costumes, revealing Hallie for the shy librarian with freckles she was— but wealthy, elegant Nick Harrington was still the baron . . . and not in her league. When Nick turned up on her doorstep in pursuit of his fantasy lady, Hallie was sure he'd discover his mistake and run for the hills!"

It's a joy for me to send you the same heartfelt wishes for the season that we've sent you every year since LOVE-SWEPT began. May your New Year be filled with all the best things in life—the company of good friends and family, peace and prosperity, and of course, love.

Warm wishes for 1988 from all of us at LOVESWEPT.

Sincerely,

Carolyn Nichols

Carolyn Nichols
  Editor

LOVESWEPT
Bantam Books, Inc.
666 Fifth Avenue
New York, NY 10103